Addie Malone, brave frontier[...]
of Shotgun Ridge in the 1800s, would be proud to
see the town's bustling rebirth. Just last year, it was
nearly extinct. But thanks to the efforts of four smug,
matchmaking old men, Shotgun Ridge was bursting
at the family seams once more. Now, it was time
for a new bachelor roundup—and sexy, flirtatious
Dr. Chance Hammond was due for a taste of his
own medicine!

* * *

Chance had thought he was perfectly happy as
a bachelor. Ever since the old folks had started
pulling their matchmaking shenanigans, he'd
had to dodge all manner of women. Then Kelly
had come to town, and he'd started to think that
bachelorhood wasn't all it was cracked up to be.

An odd pressure built up in his chest, emotions he
couldn't define, that seemed just out of reach. An
anxiety lurked inside him that made him want to
sweep Kelly off her feet and hold her to him until
he could figure it out.

The chemistry between them was undeniable. But
that didn't mean she would fall into his arms and
live happily ever after with him. Her heart had
been wounded.

Chance wanted to be the man to heal it.

Dear Reader,

Happy Holidays! Everyone at Harlequin American Romance wishes you joy and cheer at this wonderful time of year.

This month, bestselling author Judy Christenberry inaugurates MAITLAND MATERNITY: TRIPLETS, QUADS & QUINTS, our newest in-line continuity, with *Triplet Secret Babies*. In this exciting series, multiple births lead to remarkable love stories when Maitland Maternity Hospital opens a multiple birth wing. Look for *Quadruplets on the Doorstep* by Tina Leonard next month and *The McCallum Quintuplets* (3 stories in 1 volume) featuring *New York Times* bestselling author Kasey Michaels, Mindy Neff and Mary Anne Wilson in February.

In *The Doctor's Instant Family,* the latest book in Mindy Neff's BACHELORS OF SHOTGUN RIDGE miniseries, a sexy and single M.D. is intrigued by his mysterious new office assistant. Can the small-town doctor convince the single mom to trust him with her secrets—and her heart? Next, temperatures rise when a handsome modern-day swashbuckler offers to be nanny to three little girls in exchange for access to a plain-Jane professor's house in *Her Passionate Pirate* by Neesa Hart. And let us welcome a new author to the Harlequin American Romance family. Kathleen Webb makes her sparkling debut with *Cindrella's Shoe Size*.

Enjoy this month's offerings, and make sure to return each and every month to Harlequin American Romance!

Wishing you happy reading,

Melissa Jeglinski
Associate Senior Editor
Harlequin American Romance

THE DOCTOR'S
INSTANT FAMILY
Mindy Neff

HARLEQUIN®

TORONTO • NEW YORK • LONDON
AMSTERDAM • PARIS • SYDNEY • HAMBURG
STOCKHOLM • ATHENS • TOKYO • MILAN • MADRID
PRAGUE • WARSAW • BUDAPEST • AUCKLAND

This book is dedicated to Wayne and Beth Neff.
There's nothing greater than the love of family.
You guys are the best.

And to my husband, Gene,
who always comes up with the greatest scenes!

ISBN 0-373-16902-7

THE DOCTOR'S INSTANT FAMILY

Copyright © 2001 by Melinda Neff.

This edition published by arrangement with Harlequin Books S.A.

Visit us at www.eHarlequin.com

Printed in U.S.A.

ABOUT THE AUTHOR

Mindy Neff published her first book with Harlequin American Romance in 1995. Since then, she has appeared regularly on the Waldenbooks's bestseller list and won numerous awards, including the National Readers' Choice Award and the *Romantic Times Magazine* Career Achievement Award.

Originally from Louisiana, Mindy settled in Southern California, where she married a really romantic guy and raised five great kids. Family, friends, writing and reading are her passions. When not writing, Mindy's ideal getaway is a good book, hot sunshine and a chair at the river's edge at her second home in Parker, Arizona.

Mindy loves to hear from readers and can be reached at P.O. Box 2704-262, Huntington Beach, CA 92647, or through her Web site at www.mindyneff.com, or e-mail at mindyneff@aol.com.

Books by Mindy Neff

HARLEQUIN AMERICAN ROMANCE

644—A FAMILY MAN
663—ADAM'S KISS
679—THE BAD BOY NEXT DOOR
711—THEY'RE THE ONE!
739—A BACHELOR FOR THE BRIDE
759—THE COWBOY IS A DADDY
769—SUDDENLY A DADDY
795—THE VIRGIN & HER BODYGUARD*
800—THE PLAYBOY & THE MOMMY*

809—A PREGNANCY AND A PROPOSAL
830—THE RANCHER'S MAIL-ORDER
　　　BRIDE†
834—THE PLAYBOY'S OWN MISS PRIM†
838—THE HORSEMAN'S CONVENIENT
　　　WIFE†
857—THE SECRETARY GETS HER MAN
898—CHEYENNE'S LADY†
902—THE DOCTOR'S INSTANT FAMILY†

*Tall, Dark & Irresistible
†Bachelors of Shotgun Ridge

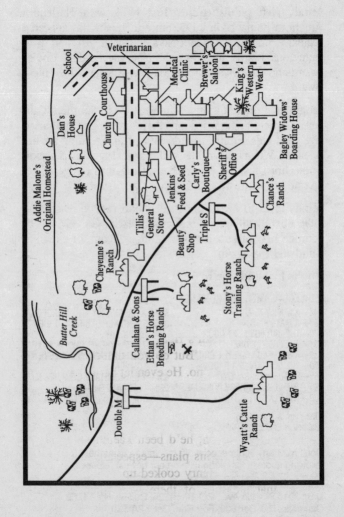

Prologue

"I tell you, some of the boys in this town just don't know a good thing when they see it!" Ozzie Peyton stoked the fire in the fireplace, satisfied with the soothing warmth that rushed through the room like a welcome burst of sunshine.

Some might call him a crazy old fool, but he liked to keep the house comfortable for his sweet Vanessa. Her portrait hung above the mantel, and though she'd gone to the hereafter several years back, she was still his best friend and confidante.

"Why, the woman's right under his nose," he lamented to Vanessa. "But do you think he'd do anything about it? Heck no. He even let her get away with staying home on Thanksgiving—but I told you about that, didn't I, love?"

He sighed and sat down with his journal. Since Vanessa had passed on, he'd been keeping a record of his daily thoughts, his plans—especially the ones he, Lloyd, Vern, and Henry cooked up.

Not that the four of them were such a devious bunch. But once they'd tried their hand at this here matchmakin' business, the excitement had simply swept them away. Nothing made a man feel better than when love was in the air.

"Families and babies, that's our aim, you bet. The sound of sweet children's voices. Kelly Anderson has two of the cutest tykes. The littlest one is so quiet." His loving gaze rested on Vanessa's smiling lips. "You'd have gentled her, love, eased out her secrets and gotten her to open up, I just know it. And it's at times like this that I miss you so much."

He told himself he wasn't going to get all maudlin. Vanessa would have his hide. She'd been a sunny woman, so filled with goodness and compassion. The good Lord had seen fit to take her too soon, in Ozzie's opinion, but he didn't like to question the Man Upstairs.

There were reasons for everything—including heartache.

"Plenty of heartache with Kelly Anderson and her little girls, I'm thinking. You remember Bill Dunaway, don't you, darlin'? He was part of my squadron back in forty-two—a young, wet-behind-the-ears medic. Kelly's his daughter, and when he called me to talk over her problems, well, it just seemed like the perfect plan to have her come on out here and work for Chance for a spell. The boy's fairly hopping in the medical arena these days."

Outside the big picture window, snowflakes drifted gently from the night sky. So far they were having a mild winter in Montana, which was practically unheard of.

"If the weather can cooperate, I don't know why the fool kids can't do the same. Why, before long, I'm thinking we're—the boys and me—are gonna just have to knock their heads together. Chance and Kelly's, that is.''

He sighed and picked up his pen. ''I know, I know, love. Subtle. I'm an ornery old cuss, though. Thought this one had just fallen plum into our laps, what with old Bill calling me out of the blue that way. I'll give them till Christmas.'' He gazed back at the portrait where dancing flames from the fireplace cast shadows over Vanessa's face, giving her the look of a Madonna.

''Wouldn't mind a little help from your department, if you know what I mean. If you could just speak to the Man Upstairs… Well, you do your best, sweetheart. After all, it's Christmastime. The season for miracles.''

Chapter One

Kelly Anderson heard the sound of sleigh bells.

"Mommy, come look!" Six-year-old Jessica snatched at the lace curtains, then abandoned her place at the front window and bounded off the couch. Four-year-old Kimberly, her round eyes filled with wonder, reached for Kelly's hand, giving a slight tug—a bid for action or protection, she couldn't tell.

It broke her heart that her youngest daughter hadn't spoken a word in six months. At one time she'd been a chatterbox just like her older sister. But tragedy had trapped her voice inside a broken little soul that hours of therapy had failed to mend.

Kelly had hoped the temporary move to Shotgun Ridge, Montana, would heal the horrors a four-year-old should never have had to witness.

They'd been here a little more than a month now, and Kimmy was still silent.

"Come on, Mom! Hurry!"

"I'm coming," she said, letting her daughters drag her out onto the front porch of Mildred and Opal Bagley's boardinghouse.

The night air was downright freezing, something

she still wasn't used to, especially coming from California's mild climate.

Her heart gave a little flip, then softened in absolute delight. A reluctant smile pulled at her mouth.

Dr. Chance Hammond, her sexy-as-sin temporary employer, was parked at the curb…in a sleigh of all things. Well, it looked like a sleigh, anyway. A sort of retrofitted hay wagon pulled by two well-behaved horses adorned with wreaths of jingling bells on their yokes.

She recalled a conversation she'd had with her father hardly a month ago. Frustrated with the turmoil her life was in, she'd wondered what had happened to the days of *Little House on the Prairie,* where neighbors helped neighbors, folks paid for medical services in chickens and homemade canned goods, and life moved at a pace where a person could at least catch her breath.

Looking at the sight before her, she decided she'd found it.

"Get your coats, ladies," Chance called, his hands holding the reins loosely. "Your chariot awaits."

"I wasn't aware I'd ordered a chariot," Kelly said.

He cocked a sexy brow and Kelly felt an unwelcome tug of response flutter in her stomach. She wasn't here to start a relationship with a man—especially a doctor—but this one was fairly persistent. Ever since she'd come to work at his small clinic, he'd made no secret of his attraction to her.

"Aw, you've forgotten already. The drive-through live nativity production starts tonight."

"I didn't forget. It's only down the street a ways."

Although the thought of walking two blocks in the snow made her shiver on general principle. Her blood had yet to thicken sufficiently. She'd been cold since she'd arrived in Montana.

"Now why would you want to walk when you've got a perfectly good sleigh and tour guide to get you there?"

"Please, Mommy?" Jessica hopped up and down. "Kimberly wants to go! She said so."

Kelly glanced down at her youngest daughter. The little girl hadn't uttered a word, but that didn't stop Jessica from claiming to know her sister's mind. Kimberly chose not to use her vocal cords, but her eyes spoke volumes.

And Kelly would do anything to hear that sweet voice once again.

She looked back at Chance. "All right. Give me a minute to get our coats."

He gave her a grin that made her nerves skitter in a way they hadn't in a very long time, a grin that reminded her of the wolf in one of the fairy tales she read to her girls. Well, he'd just have to turn that charm on someone else.

She wasn't taking up with Dr. Chance Hammond, and she wasn't letting him figuratively walk her through the woods to Grandma's house.

She would, however, accept a short ride to the church's drive-through nativity production.

For her daughters, she told herself.

After bundling against the weather in gloves, scarves and heavy coats, she herded Jessica and Kimberly out to the sleigh.

Chance hopped down and lifted each of the girls into the wagon, then turned to Kelly, reaching out.

She sidestepped him. "I think I can manage."

He shook his head. "My mama taught me to be chivalrous to the ladies."

He put his hands at her waist, and she gripped his arms, looking up into his laughing eyes. "Your mama teach you to flirt, too?"

A few gentle flakes of snow drifted onto his hat. He winked. "This isn't flirting, Hollywood. When I decide to flirt, you'll definitely know."

Oh, he was so smooth. And so charming. And ever since she'd told him she'd come from Beverly Hills, he'd been calling her Hollywood. She'd quit correcting him after the first couple of days at the clinic. "Are those sheep's clothes under that coat?"

He laughed. "Now the woman calls me a wolf."

"Did I, now?" She shouldn't be standing in the freezing cold, gazing up at him like a young girl in her first blush of a crush, but she couldn't help it. Chance Hammond was a difficult man to resist.

"Implied," he corrected himself. "And they're shepherd's clothes, thank you so much for noticing. I'm in charge of the donkeys." Beneath his coat was a flowing white costume that didn't quite reach the hem of his jeans.

"Don't shepherds watch the sheep?"

"Wyatt Malone's in charge of them. Him being a cattleman and all, he wants to keep a close eye on the critters for fear they'll get loose and mow his grazing land down to the roots."

"In this snow?"

Chance shrugged and hoisted her into the sleigh, grinning at her surprised gasp. "Those cattlemen haven't met a sheep yet they trust."

Yes, well, Kelly wasn't too trusting of this particular shepherd, either.

He vaulted up on the seat, glanced back at Jessica and Kimberly. "Ready, girls?" When they nodded happily, he clicked his tongue at the horses and set them moving slowly down Main Street.

Kelly felt the bite of frigid air against her cheeks. Christmas was definitely in the air. The night was so clear she could see for miles across the prairie as she glanced back over her shoulder, away from town.

Facing forward again, listening to the merry jingle of the bells on the horses, Kelly took in the sights and sounds. They had an otherworldly feel, far removed from anything she'd ever experienced.

The town was breathtakingly beautiful. Christmas lights twinkled in candy colors of red, green, blue and orange, strung along every available length of eaves on the storefronts they passed.

Carly McCall's boutique windows glittered with shiny baubles and balls draped on mannequins adorned in old-fashioned lace and velvet. Buttons and trim and all manner of sewing notions lay scattered against cotton batting that resembled fresh-fallen snow.

At the end of Main Street, a twenty-foot decorated Douglas fir straddled the courthouse and churchyard, a bright star at its highest point.

Cars were already lined up behind a barricade

guarded by one of Sheriff Cheyenne Bodine's deputies.

"My gosh, I didn't know this was going to be such a huge production," Kelly said.

"Compliments of Emily Bodine," Chance said. "The woman knows her business when it comes to advertising."

"I'll say." Kelly had just started working at the clinic when Emily had come to town, pregnant with twins as the result of a surrogate agreement with her sister and Cheyenne Bodine's brother. The woman's capacity to love touched Kelly and everyone else in town—especially the man who'd become Emily's handsome husband, Sheriff Cheyenne Bodine.

"A camel!" Jessica squealed from behind them, bouncing just behind Chance's shoulder. "Look, Kimmy!"

Both little girls poked their heads between Chance and Kelly, their round eyes agog.

"Pretty cool, huh?" Chance said with a wink. "Ethan Callahan had the camels and donkeys trucked in, Wyatt Malone provided the cows and sheep, and Stony Stratton brought horses."

They'd barely pulled the sleigh off to the side of the church before Jessica and Kimberly were clamoring to get down.

"Careful, girls," Kelly cautioned. "We don't want to spook the animals."

"Can we pet 'em?" Jessica asked while Kimberly's eyes pleaded.

"'Course you can pet them," Chance said. "As

long as your mom or me are with you. Careful of the camels, though. They spit.''

''Do not!''

He grinned, winked at Jessica and ruffled Kimmy's hair. ''Scout's honor.''

Kelly raised a brow. ''Were you a Scout?''

''Well, no. But they do spit—the camels, that is.''

He took off his coat and Kelly smiled at his shepherd costume. He was likely to freeze his buns off in this weather. Since they were nice buns, she thought that'd be a pity.

''Silent Night'' played through huge speakers positioned on the church steps. A tent with portable heaters housed tables laden with cookies, hot chocolate and urns of steaming coffee.

''I need my shepherds in place!'' Dan Lucas called. The pastor's booming laughter rang around the parking lot, vying with the sounds of animals, children and Christmas hymns.

''That's me,'' Chance said. ''Coming?''

Kelly shook her head. ''We're not in costume. I'll catch you on your break.''

''Aw, Mom,'' Jessica complained.

''Plenty of time to visit with the animals and do a walk-through,'' she told her daughter. ''We'll go help out at the concession stand for a while.''

Chance nodded and headed for his place, taking the lead ropes of the donkeys he was in charge of.

Kelly watched him go, admiring his grace, his height, his willingness to participate. Even wearing a shepherd's robe, there was no denying the man's masculinity. He radiated it like a beacon. Which made his charm all the more appealing.

Oh, she knew there was an attraction between them—she'd have to be blind to miss it. But she'd made it clear right from the get-go that she wasn't interested in a relationship.

Kimberly and Jessica had to be her first priority. Life had turned upside down for them all during the past year.

This was a stopover, a chance to heal, a chance to rethink and regroup.

And as much as her battered feminine soul wanted to answer the call of Chance Hammond's flirtations, she knew she had to resist.

Holding her hands out for Jessica and Kimberly, she made her way over to the concession stand just as cars were beginning to turn into the church parking lot. They would make the loop from Main Street through the church lot, driving slowly to take in the live nativity and listen to the Christmas hymns. If they wanted, they could stop at the refreshment stand for a hot drink passed through the car window.

Iris Brewer, who owned Brewer's Saloon in town, looked up from pouring steaming coffee into a plastic cup.

"Well hello, there, loves. Did Mildred and Opal come with you all?"

"No," Kelly said. "They claimed their bones weren't up to standing in the cold half the night. They'll be along later, though."

Mildred and Opal Bagley were widowed sisters who owned the boardinghouse where Kelly was staying.

The sisters were characters, fond of bickering good-naturedly, yet were as sweet and welcoming as you could ask for. But Kelly knew she needed to find other housing. In another week or so, extended families would start showing up for the holiday celebrations, and since the new hotel wasn't built yet, the Bagley widows' boardinghouse was going to be bursting at the seams.

"Can we help out?" Kelly asked Iris.

"Of course. I'll hand you the coffee and hot chocolate, and you can pass it right through the car windows. The little ones can help with the cookies, but mind that you stay close to your mom," she cautioned them. "No getting toes under the tires, you hear?"

Jessica and Kimberly were happy to have a job and puffed up their little chests importantly.

"We don't see much of you, Kelly," Vera Tillis commented as she lined up to wish the cruisers a merry Christmas and smile at excited children bouncing in the back seats of the cars. "I trust you got over your bug?"

Kelly pulled the collar of her coat higher around her chin, not only to ward off the icy-cold air, but to hide.

"Um, I'm fine. Thank you for asking." She'd told an outright fib when Chance had asked her to join him at one of the neighbor's houses on Thanksgiving.

Somehow, though, the man made even a simple request for a patient consult sound like a date. Socializing outside of work was simply too risky.

Tonight, she'd had little choice. He'd been sneaky, brought the sleigh and appealed to Jessica and Kimberly, knowing full well the girls would sway her decision.

She'd have looked like a mean old witch if she'd refused to go with him.

Besides, there was no sense in her daughters suffering because she was worried about keeping a lid on her emotions. Soon enough, Chance would get tired of the chase and give up on her. Men usually did when something wasn't serving their needs. She ought to know.

A steady stream of cars lined the streets of the town, and after a while, Kelly forgot all about being cold. They'd gone through several urns of coffee and cocoa, and backup pots were already brewing.

"Can we go look at the baby Jesus and camels now?" Jessica asked.

"Yes, do go," Iris encouraged. "I see Mildred and Opal headed up the walk. They'll take over for you."

Kelly adjusted Kimberly's scarf, tucking it more snugly around her neck, buttoned Jessica's coat and gave a warning look when the little girl started to complain, then held out her hands, holding both her daughters close to her side as they slipped between cars and moved toward the nativity scene.

A huge crèche, built by the town's contractor, Jake McCall, was the focal point of the production, a bright star seemingly floating several feet above the wooden structure. One of the new babies in town—Kelly wasn't sure which, Eden's, Dora's or one of Emily's twins—was being lowered into a bed of straw. Probably one of the twins, because Emily was stepping in to play the part of Mary, and her husband, Cheyenne, was dressed as Joseph, gazing in wonder at the baby in the manger.

People from all over the county and as far away as Miles City and Billings lined the streets with cars and pickups, cruising by to view the Christmas scene.

One of the camels, an impressive seven feet in height, was standing and looking bored half to death. Another was kneeling, its knobby knees bent, long eyelashes fanning its eyes. Portable heaters kept the set warm, and the cabin-size wood structure kept stray snow flurries off the cast of characters.

Chance held the lead ropes of two donkeys. He looked up and saw her coming, spoke to Wyatt Malone—who was indeed minding the sheep with an eagle eye—then handed one of the donkeys off to his friend and moved around behind the crèche motioning for Kelly to follow.

"How's it going, Hollywood?"

She shivered inside her jacket. "Freezing."

"Aw, this is mild. Wait'll we get a blizzard—" he winked "—and we have to make a house call."

"I think I can wait." That was another thing that made her feel as though she'd stepped back in time. House calls. Where she came from, that was unheard of. But they were very much a part of Chance Hammond's medical practice.

Jessica whispered something to Kimberly, and both little girls gazed at the top of the Christmas tree several yards away, then looked above the crèche to the Star of Bethlehem suspended by wires.

"Do you believe in angels?" Jessica asked Chance. He smiled. "Sure."

"Did you *see* her?"

"Yep."

"No. Not the toy one on the tree," Jessica insisted.

"Oh. You mean the ones over there?" He pointed to where a choir of angels were singing Christmas hymns, flashlights hidden beneath their silver wings to give a glow to the wings and halos.

"No, the *real* one."

"Jess," Kelly cautioned when her daughter's voice raised an octave in impatience.

Chance winked. "I guess I didn't see her, then. Probably only special little girls get to see real ones."

Kimberly looked at him, her eyes as solemn as his tone. He reached out and trailed a gentle finger over her cheek.

Passing the donkey's lead rope to Kelly, he said, "Can you hold this for a second?"

Kelly didn't want the responsibility, but the rope was already in her hands before she could object. Her insides quivered with nerves. She'd heard that animals could sense when someone was afraid, so she did her best to bluff, to pretend that she stood chest to nose with donkeys every day of her life.

She watched Chance as he bent down to inspect the hem of his shepherd costume where a tear in the shape of his boot heel had rent the fabric. Rather than dwell on the proximity of the donkey's teeth to her sweater, she focused on Chance's long fingers. She imagined they could probably stitch a torn seam in fabric as well as they could a life-threatening laceration in skin. He was an excellent doctor.

She glanced up just as an old Buick pulled away

from the crèche on its way to make the loop of the church parking lot. Suddenly the car backfired. The explosion of sound ripped through the crèche, setting off a chain reaction that resembled a slow motion free-for-all.

Voices shouted and soothed as animals shied.

The donkey Kelly was holding lunged, nearly knocking her over, and kicked out with his hind legs.

"Watch out!" She shoved Jessica and Kimberly back, but the warning wasn't quick enough for Chance.

He gave a startled yelp as the animal's hoof connected with his temple, knocking him flat on his back where he lay unmoving. Unconscious.

Stony Stratton was at Kelly's side in an instant, taking the reins of the donkey, speaking gently to the animal and getting him back under control.

She rushed to Chance, kneeling in the snow, checking his pulse, the gash on his head. She was only vaguely aware of the crowd that had gathered around them. Her sole focus was on Chance, and she mentally blocked offers of help and words of concern.

"Chance." She called his name loudly, held her hand on his chest when he stirred and tried to sit up. "Stay put."

"What…?"

"Just be still, would you?" Her heart raced, but her hands were steady as a rock as she assessed his injuries, applied pressure to the wound, dug a penlight out of her pocket and shone it in his eyes to check the reaction of his pupils.

"I'm okay," Chance protested. "Just give me a—"

"Hush."

Jessica, disobeying the directive to stay back, peered at the wound like a bloodthirsty ghoul.

"Ew, he's got a big owie. Kimmy, come look."

"Girls, Chance doesn't need an audience." She glanced up at Stony and Cheyenne, who were sticking close in case she needed help, but keeping the crowd at bay to give her room.

"It's not that bad," she said. "Go ahead with the production. I'll shout if I need a hand." Since they were actually behind the crèche, they had a certain amount of privacy from the cars that had come to a halt when the animals had nearly bolted.

Everyone except Jessica and Kimberly moved away. Kelly scooped up a clean patch of snow and used it to wipe away some of the blood around Chance's wound, being careful not to contaminate the actual site.

"Don't worry," Jessica said compassionately, patting Chance on the shoulder. "Mommy can fix your hurt."

"She can, huh?"

"Yep." Jessica looked back at Kelly, pride shining in her big blue eyes. Kelly had an idea what was coming and didn't quite know how to head it off.

"*Now* is it okay to say you're a doctor, Mommy?"

Like a slow-moving spotlight, Chance's gaze slid up to hers. Confusion and surprise covered the embarrassed discomfort that had been in his eyes a moment ago.

"A doctor," he repeated.

Kelly sighed. She felt guilty as hell asking her oldest daughter to keep silent about her profession. It wasn't really a secret. She simply hadn't wanted to resurrect the responsibilities she'd left behind in California, hadn't wanted to deal with the questions and explanations.

Her private life was hers. She wasn't here to be a doctor.

Still, it made her feel bad that she'd advised her daughter not to mention the details, especially since Jessica was perfectly capable of speaking, and Kimberly, though capable, *wouldn't* speak.

Chapter Two

"You want to run that by me again?" Chance asked, feeling as if the kick in the head had scrambled his brains. He flinched and tried to evade her when she wiped more freezing snow over his temple, then pressed a handkerchief against his wound.

"I'm a doctor. And the best you've got right now, ace, so stay still and quit being a baby."

Jessica obviously thought it was hysterically funny that her mother had called him a baby, because she fell over laughing.

Chance glanced at Kimberly. He'd be happy to be the butt of a joke if it made the youngest girl respond. A smile peeked out, puffing out her chubby cheeks. But no sound.

He looked back at Kelly, who was going through all the motions he would have as a certified family physician when assessing an injury.

He arched a brow, an action that brought a stinging pain to his wound. "Ouch, damn it."

Kimberly shook her head, her round eyes filled with life, but her mouth silent.

Jessica translated. "You're not supposed to say naughty words. The angel will cry."

"Say's who?"

"The angel, silly."

Kelly brushed a hand gently over her daughter's hair and looked down at Chance—a little guiltily, he thought. Why had she kept her credentials from him? Not that he'd ever asked her to perform any duties that would risk his own medical license.

And why in the world did this kid keep harping on angels as though there was a real one shining in their midst? His head was starting to ache like a kick in the head ought to, and he was feeling decidedly unsettled.

"She talks to an angel," Kelly explained softly, answering his unspoken question. "They both do, although Kimmy doesn't use words."

The look on her face as she revealed what he'd already figured out about the angel touched a soft chord in him. A mother's fierce protection, a plea for understanding.

There was more to this family than Kelly allowed people to see.

In the month she'd been working at his clinic, he knew little more than her name, that she was as efficient as all get-out, and that she made him burn.

It was the damnedest thing. When she'd first arrived in town, he'd hired her on the spot and within a week, despite her "no trespassing" demeanor, his gut told him she was someone special. So he'd asked her out on a date. She'd refused, of course, but the chemistry between them during working hours had been white-hot, had fairly palpitated in the air.

He'd come within a hairbreadth of kissing her, right there in the storage room amid drug samples, gauze, bedpans and the copying machine.

All it had taken was the mere brush of their bodies, and the earth had shifted beneath his feet.

Evidently Kelly hadn't experienced the same phenomenon, because she still refused to go out with him.

Although it nearly killed him, Chance had tried to put his baser instincts on the back burner, deciding they could work together without hormones coming between them. They were adults. And with the town fairly bursting at the seams—thanks in great part to the matchmakers—he desperately needed her help at the clinic.

In a panic when his previous nurse had left, Kelly had been a godsend. He'd originally hired her as his receptionist, but when the office had been overrun one day with patients, she'd jumped right in, taking vital signs, recording patient histories and handling the preliminaries. Amongst the chaos, he recalled commenting that she obviously had training. She'd merely answered yes, and they'd left it at that.

Now he realized she was probably overqualified for the job.

"Can you stand on your own?" Kelly asked, bringing his thoughts back to the unsettling situation at hand. "We need to get you across the street to the clinic so we can stitch this laceration."

He saw a couple of his buddies moving in to help him to his feet and waved them off. His pride was smarting enough as it was.

"Yeah, I can stand." He got to his feet, disgusted

when he actually swayed and she reached out for his arm.

"Macho man," she murmured. "It won't kill you to lean on me."

That's what *she* thought. All he would have to do was ease up to that soft body, and his own would go embarrassingly hard. "I can walk."

"Then let's get to it."

"Why don't you leave the girls with us?" Stony offered, having moved closer despite Chance's blatant body language discouraging it. Hell, whatever happened to the silently understood male code that most guys respected, giving a buddy plenty of room when it was clear his manliness was challenged?

Stony Stratton, a man usually stingy with his smiles, grinned like a loon as he gazed steadily at Chance. "Eden and I will keep an eye on Jessica and Kimmy, let them visit with the animals."

"Are you sure?" Kelly asked, obviously torn about letting her daughters out of her sight.

That was another thing she'd been diligent about since she'd come to town. Keeping to herself. Keeping her girls close by. A loner who'd watched from afar.

Chance decided he'd had about enough of it.

He wanted some answers—albeit a bit late in the game. And he wanted Kelly Anderson.

In what capacity, he wasn't sure. He only knew that he hadn't felt this way about a woman since his failed engagement to Dana in medical school.

And though that scared him plenty, it also stung his ego.

Because she went out of her way not to notice.

Man alive, he was losing his touch with the ladies, that was for sure. It grated even more that the old fellows in town were vocally, heartlessly, pointing that out at every opportunity.

"We'd be happy to watch the kids for you," Eden said, coming to stand beside her husband. "They'll be fine, Kelly. In fact, why don't you let them spend the night at our place? Nikki's been dying for company."

"Oh, I don't know, they don't have clothes or—"

"Please!" Nikki begged, reaching out to link hands with both Jessica and Kimberly. "I got *piles* of clothes. And I got new dishes and Rosie eats all the sugar at the tea parties."

"Rosie's the dog," Chance explained.

"Yeah, Mom. Please?" Jessica begged.

Reluctance was keen in Kelly's eyes, but once she looked at the hopeful expressions on all three little girls' faces, she nodded.

"Great," Eden said. "You go take care of Chance's head and don't worry about a thing." She ushered the kids off, admonishing everyone to get back in place so the program could continue before the line of cars stretched clear to Wyoming.

Chance gazed down at Kelly. "Yeah, Doc, take care of my head." He eased an arm around her shoulders, felt her stiffen. "Don't want me to fall on my butt again, do you?"

"Pretty cocky for a man who's white as that sheet you're wearing. Come on, cowboy. I think I'm going to enjoy sticking needles in your head."

He'd forgotten about that part of it and groaned.

The clinic, across the street from the church, was

only a short walk. Slushy snow grooved by tire tracks, formed twin parallel mounds on both sides of the blacktop. Cars and pickups, with snow piled on bumpers and sticking to mud flaps, were parked diagonally at the curb.

Using his key, Chance unlocked the door and turned on the lights. The smell of antiseptic and adhesive permeated the air, familiar scents that were as much a part of his world as the smell of springtime or his mother's apple pie.

Anxious to check out the cut on his head himself, he went to a mirror and inspected the wound, still thoroughly annoyed that he'd let the accident happen in the first place. He knew better than to get behind an animal the way he had.

"Think you can sew it up on your own?" Kelly asked as she waited patiently for him to step away from the mirror.

"Maybe it doesn't need stitches."

She sighed and shook her head. "The curse of a doctor. Wants to diagnose himself. You make the worse kind of patient."

"Well, how many times have *you* had stitches?"

"Twice." She held up her left palm, showing him both of the scars within inches of each other. "Had a run-in with a chisel in high school wood shop. The other's where I slipped with a scalpel in biology lab."

"Ouch. Not a great recommendation from where I'm sitting."

She raised a brow. "That was ages ago in high school and med school. I've improved some since then. Besides, that donkey did a fine job of opening up your head, so there'll be no need for me to pick up a scalpel. Now will you sit down before you fall? You look like you're going to faint.''

"I'm not going to faint." He hadn't meant to sound so indignant.

"Such a tough guy." She moved around the room, gathering disinfectant, sterile drapes, gloves, a syringe, needle and suture thread.

Chance took off his coat and the shepherd costume, then eased a hip onto the fresh sheet of sterile paper covering the examining table, watching the efficient way Kelly moved.

He usually saw her in nursing clothes, her hair held back in a bun or a clip. Tonight she wore figure-hugging designer jeans, a soft wool sweater that barely reached the waistband of her jeans, and trendy chunky boots.

Her dark-blond hair hung loose around her shoulders, the overhead lamp picking up the shifting highlights. Her full lips had a natural pink tint, enhanced by gloss.

A mouth made for slow deep kisses.

Oh, man. He shifted on the table, crinkling the paper covering, trying to stop those kinds of thoughts. But a thousand questions were racing through his mind.

She lined up instruments on a sterile drape atop a stainless steel tray, then opened the drug cabinet and made her selection with hardly a second glance.

Why hadn't he seen the signs sooner? He'd felt lucky to have her, marveled at her efficiency, but he'd never suspected Kelly Anderson was a doctor.

She put on a lab coat, scrubbed her hands and

snapped on a pair of gloves. Turning, she caught him staring.

"Why would you pass yourself off as an assistant when you're a doctor?"

"I have my reasons."

"Obviously. I'm asking you to share them."

"You want to lie down so we can get this over with?"

He arched a brow, swore when the movement made his wound sting, then managed a grin. "A beautiful woman asks me to lie down, then in the same breath wants to get it over with. We could spend an evening making something of that statement, Hollywood."

She waited until he obeyed her directive, then set about cleansing the wound. "You ought to be worried about my sewing skills, not thinking about sex."

"Just looking at you makes me think about sex." The antiseptic on the laceration stung, and he flinched.

"Sorry," she murmured. "You really want to keep up this particular line of conversation?"

"Make you nervous?"

She gave him a direct look, set down the swab and picked up a syringe. "I haven't had sex in well over a year. You being a doctor and all, I think you probably covered the same psych courses I did, know the body's typical reaction to visual, oral or mental stimulus. Whether I want to have sex with you or not, I'm likely to tremble nonetheless just from the direction of this conversation. Seeing as I'm the one in control of the stitches and the size of your scar, do you want to take that chance? Close your eyes—this is going to hurt a little."

He didn't heed her directive, but kept his gaze firmly on hers. "Why do I think you're going to enjoy inflicting that hurt?"

She smiled and injected anesthetic in several spots around the wound.

She had a gentle touch, but it was still painful, and Chance decided he was going to be more conscious of his patients' feelings from now on. He'd gotten so used to dispensing medical care, he rarely thought about what the person on the receiving end actually felt.

Oh, he knew certain procedures hurt. But it was one thing to *tell* someone something was going to sting, and quite another to actually *feel* that sting.

She set the syringe aside and sat down on a rolling stool, giving the medication a chance to numb.

"So, how'd you end up in Shotgun Ridge?" he asked. *And why haven't you had sex in more than a year?*

"My father is a friend of Ozzie Peyton's."

"I might have known. I figured something was up with those old guys."

"You know my father?"

"No. I meant Ozzie, Lloyd Brewer, Vern Tillis and Henry Jenkins. The town matchmakers."

"What do they have to do with my dad? And matchmaking?"

"I've had a sneaking suspicion for a while now that I was their next target. I think you got caught in the crossfire if your dad was conversing with Ozzie. They sent you to me."

She looked away and her eyes went incredibly sad.

"I don't think so. My dad knows I'm not looking for a relationship. I just went through a trying one."

"Divorce?"

"Death."

"Oh, man. I'm sorry." He'd assumed she was divorced. And now he felt bad about coming on to her so strongly over the past month. He'd known there were secrets in her life, but he'd had no idea she might be mourning a husband. In his own defense, he reminded himself that he *had* asked about her marital status. She'd emphatically told him there was no man in her life and she wanted to keep it that way.

She acknowledged his sympathy with a nod, then rose and probed at the skin around his wound. "How's it feeling?"

"Getting numb."

"We'll give it another minute or two."

"How long ago did your husband die?"

"Six months."

"That's rough. For you and your girls."

She leaned a hip against the examining table, gazed down at him. "That's part of the reason I'm here."

"To heal?"

"For the girls to heal. Kimmy saw her father die. She hasn't spoken since."

Chance swore. "Nobody should witness that, especially a child. How did it happen?"

"Electrocution. He was using a faulty drill motor and had the bad sense to ground himself against a metal pipe."

She said it matter-of-factly, but the stark pain that flashed in her eyes told a different story. He reached out and touched the thick wool fabric of her sleeve where her lab coat had ridden up. "Kelly, I'm so sorry."

"Yeah, me, too." She probed his wound again. "You'll probably have a scar. I'll take small stitches, though, and we'll hold our breath." She paused with the needle suspended above his brow. "Don't frown. I really am good at this."

"That's not why I'm frowning."

She sighed. "I know."

Covering his face with a drape, leaving only a small opening where the laceration was exposed, he felt the slight numbed tug as she took small stitches, using a silk so fine it would hardly be seen.

Her concentration was complete; even though Chance couldn't see her face, he knew it. He could tell by the shift of her body, the competence of her hands, that she knew her business, could probably do these stitches in her sleep. Silence surrounded them, broken only by the whisper of fabric and the clink of metal against metal as instruments were picked up and laid down again.

She smelled like crisp fresh air, Betadine solution and a subtle hint of floral perfume.

He wanted to reach out and take her in his arms, hated being out of control this way, hated that someone else was taking care of him. *He* was the caregiver. The healer.

And Kelly needed care, even though he knew she would deny it. She needed arms around her. He had an idea there was much more to her story than she let on. The undercurrents of what she'd left unsaid fairly shouted.

"All done," Kelly announced. "The donkey was polite. He put his hoof in just the right place. I didn't even have to shave off your eyebrow or any hair."

Chance sat up slowly, testing his reaction. "I don't know if I'd call the thing polite or not."

Kelly checked his pulse, shone a light in his eyes, then dressed his wound. "How are you feeling? Any dizziness? Nausea?"

"I'm fine." He wanted to forget this whole donkey incident as quickly as possible. "Can I ask you something personal?"

"You can ask. No guarantee I'll answer."

"I'm kind of hung up on that statement about sex you made. You said it'd been well over a year. You meant six months, right?"

She gave him a look filled with disappointment. "Please tell me you're not one of those guys who think every divorced or widowed woman is hard up for sex and is an easy target."

"Damn it, you know me better than that."

The defensiveness drained out of her like the release of a blood-pressure cuff. Her shoulders sagged as though the burdens were too heavy to hold.

"Steve lost interest in intimacy months before he died. At least with me. Turns out he was getting his needs satisfied elsewhere—with my best friend."

"Ah, hell."

She shrugged off his commiseration as though she'd shut the door on that chapter of her life and never intended to open it again. And judging by the now-rigid angle of her shoulders and the slight lift of her chin, he knew better than to push for more on that bombshell she'd just dropped.

"You could have a slight concussion," she said. "Is there someone who can stay with you tonight?"

It took a moment for him to switch conversational gears. He'd all but forgotten his injury.

Despite her professional no-nonsense tone, vulnerability radiated from her. She'd kept to herself and been so independent since she'd come to Shotgun Ridge that he couldn't bear the thought of her isolating herself again tonight. Especially since Jessica and Kimberly were spending the night at the Strattons. Kelly would be totally alone.

"You could stay with me," he suggested.

"I wasn't offering."

"As my doctor, don't you think it'd be a good idea?"

"You're pushing it, ace." But her medical training was obviously at war with her good sense. "Seriously, is there someone you can call?"

"No. Come home with me." *Let me take care of you.*

"Said the spider to the fly. I'll make some calls."

"Folks have got their own families to tend to."

"What about your family?" she asked.

"They live in Helena."

"Mmm, that's a pretty long drive."

"Yeah, and I probably shouldn't get behind the wheel just now. Maybe you could run me home."

"I don't know how to drive a sleigh."

He smiled at her slight hesitation. She was close to surrendering. "My truck's out back. Cheyenne brought the sleigh into town. I borrowed it to come pick you up.''

"So I wasn't actually on your way, was I.''

"I don't recall telling you that you were. If I remember, I said your chariot was waiting.'' He saw her chest rise as she took a deep breath.

"You'll probably be all right on your own. Though the brief loss of consciousness you had worries me some.''

"I like that you're worried about me," he said softly.

"Chance." Her tone held a warning.

He didn't heed it. "As doctors, you and I both know the odds of complications are slim. But would we take the risk if the circumstances were different? I imagine if I was the attending physician, I'd suggest an overnight hospital stay if my patient didn't have family to monitor him.''

She folded her arms beneath her breasts. "Want me to run you into Billings and check you in?''

He grinned. "My place is closer. And I happen to like your bedside manner.''

"You're not helping your case, talking like that.''

"I know." His expression cleared, all the flirting gone. "I shouldn't be baiting you like this, after...well, I'm sorry." He eased down off the examining table, stood and swayed a bit.

She reached out to steady him. "Hand over the keys, Hammond.''

"I'm okay.''

"Yeah, and I'm going to make sure you stay that way through the night. Do you have a spare bedroom?''

"Five of them."

"Five?"

"I know. Big place for just me to rattle around in."

"Have you ever...lived with anyone?"

"Been married, you mean? No."

"Smart man. Let's go."

He touched her shoulder. "You're bitter."

"Bitter's not the right word. Wiser, I guess. Surprised I could make such a huge mistake. Devastated that my children are suffering and I can't fix it. I know where I've been, Chance. And I know where I'm going—for the next little while, at least. I've got two children to take care of. They're my sole focus. I've pinned my hopes on this town. Tonight, your injury aside, makes me believe I've made the right choice, that I'm on the right road. The girls came alive this evening. I realize I've been keeping to myself since I've been here, and that's the wrong thing to do. I've got to get involved a little, get *them* involved. Something's got to click with Kimmy. It just has to."

Despite his intention otherwise, he drew her into his arms. He felt her stiffen, and soothed her. "Shh. Everybody needs a hug now and again. And since my head's hurting like a son of a gun, I figure I needed one."

She gave a muffled laugh against his shoulder. "You're so full of it, Doc."

"Yeah." He eased her away. "Thanks for the hug, Doc."

She gazed at him for a long moment. "You're welcome. Now give me your truck keys so I can get you home."

Chapter Three

Chance's house was bigger than Kelly's expensive bungalow in Beverly Hills. The price tag on her three-bedroom place was close to a million. If you plunked this house anywhere in Southern California, it would cost at least five times that, way more than she could afford.

Several acres of property housed the sprawling brick house, stables, winter-bare trees and what looked like a frozen stream that meandered parallel to the long driveway.

She parked Chance's truck in the garage and reached over to lay a hand on his arm. "We're here."

He sat up and tugged at his hat. "Did I nod off?"

"Just for a few minutes."

"Sorry about that. Let's go inside where it's not so cold."

Kelly liked the interior of the house as much as the exterior. The rooms were spacious, with comfortable leather furniture, wood floors and bookshelves holding medical reference books, as well as the latest bestsellers. He had beautiful artwork on the walls—whimsical fairies painted on canvas. Not what she would have expected. She recognized the artist's work. She'd always admired Judith Hammond's style...

"Hammond?" she said aloud.

"My mom."

"Good heavens, she's famous."

He grinned. "Yeah, but I try not to let it go to my head."

When he grinned like that, he was simply too charming. So she looked away, hiding her own smile, and continued to assess the room. On every available surface were framed photographs—a lot of them babies. Another surprise. She went over to examine the ones that rested atop the upright piano.

"Those are kids I've delivered."

"Mmm." There were names on each photo, some in standard frames, others framed with artistic flair, and always a personal note of thanks to Dr. Hammond.

What would it be like, she wondered, to walk through town and see all the children you'd helped bring into the world? Watch them grow and flourish, face heartache and joy? See them take their first steps, attend their first day of school, their first prom, experience their first brush with love?

She could hardly imagine a scenario like that in Los Angeles.

But she wasn't in Los Angeles now. She was in a quaint town where neighbors all seemed like one big family, and the town doctor proudly displayed pictures of babies as though they were much-loved nieces and nephews.

A pang of longing swept over her, and Kelly set

down the framed photo. She glanced up as Chance bent over to stoke the fire in the fireplace.

"Why don't you sit down and let me do that?"

"I'm not an invalid."

"No, but you thought you needed looking after."

"So did you," he reminded.

"Then that puts me in charge." She took the brass fireplace poker from him and urged him toward the cushy leather chair. "Sit."

"Bossy woman," he murmured, but obeyed. "I can't believe I let this happen. I work with animals all the time."

She smiled. "Four-legged or two?"

"Both. I've handled my share of mean drunks. I've also been known to stand in for the vet in a pinch—and vice versa."

She eased down on the cushions of the sofa. "I actually saved a kitten once. I was working the E.R. and the paramedics brought a family in from a fire. The little boy was clutching a kitten. The medics hadn't had a chance to see to the animal because their hands were full. I put an oxygen mask over its little mouth and did finger CPR. It was incredible."

Chance leaned his head back against the chair, watching her with a gentle smile on his face. "Doesn't matter what kind of life it is, saving them is why we're in this business, isn't it?"

"For most." Her husband hadn't shared that sentiment.

"Do you have your own practice back in California?"

Kelly nodded. "I'm an orthopedic surgeon. I specialize in kids.'' She could fix a child's bones, but she couldn't repair her daughter's soul. If only Kimberly's problems were the kind that could be seen by an X ray. If only. If only. It seemed she was thinking that a lot lately.

''If you don't mind my saying so, you look a bit young to have completed the years of training required for a specialty.''

''I'm thirty-two.'' He probably already knew that from the employment application she'd filled out when she'd applied for the job at the clinic. ''I pretty much skipped high school, graduated from college when I was eighteen and went right into med school at UCLA.''

He stared at her for a minute. She was used to that reaction, though she hadn't encountered it in a while.

''You were one of those child prodigies.''

''That's me. I was doing calculus when the rest of the girls my age were still playing with dolls.''

''Was that hard on you?''

''As a kid, yes. As an adult it became less of an issue.''

''So you've been doing this for a while. That's a lot to walk away from.''

''My kids are worth much more than any career.'' She usually kept her private business to herself, but she needed him to understand her circumstances, to understand why there wasn't room in her life to act on this attraction brewing between them.

''Steve—my husband—was a doctor, too. A well-known plastic surgeon. Since he hobnobbed with movie stars, that made him newsworthy, which made his death a circus. The media frenzy was ugly. I had to get the girls away from it—especially once the paparazzi found out that Kimmy had seen the accident.

"I thought it would blow over, but it didn't. They camped out in my front yard, just waiting for a photo opportunity. It got to where I had to keep the kids cooped up inside so we wouldn't see their faces splashed on some tabloid at the supermarket. And each day, Kimmy seemed to withdraw further into herself."

The flames in the fireplace danced as the wood crackled. A log spit, shooting a shower of embers up the flue.

"My dad suggested I come to Shotgun Ridge. And I'm glad he did. It's totally different here than in California. I wanted a slower pace, more community spirit. It's hard to explain. I wanted the girls and me to experience something new. And different."

"For a woman wanting community spirit, you've mostly kept to yourself since you've been here."

"I know. I guess I went through a bit of culture shock in the beginning. I don't know how to mingle like you all do, how to join in."

"It's simple. You just do it."

"Easy words coming from a man who's lived here all his life."

"I'll be happy to tutor you." The words were said with just a hint of suggestion.

Kelly laughed, surprised that she felt so relaxed. She should have been on guard, but she couldn't seem to keep her shield up around Chance Hammond.

He was simply too endearing, too charming and,

hands down, one of the handsomest men she'd ever seen.

He was a healer, like her, but there was an air of mystique about him, as well.

A cowboy mystique.

A very heady combination.

KELLY THOUGHT she heard the phone ring, but was too tired to do anything about it, hoping it was just a hazy part of her dream.

The next thing she knew, someone was knocking on the door. Disoriented, she came straight up off the couch, listening for the sound of ambulance sirens, emergency workers barking orders and calling for doctors.

It took a minute to realize she was still at Chance's house, not a medical resident doing E.R. rotation on two hours of sleep.

Lord, it'd been a while since she'd flashed back on those hellish days.

Probably the unfamiliar surroundings. She certainly hadn't planned to spend the whole night here. Once she'd finally talked Chance into going to bed, she'd fallen asleep on the couch, waking several times to check on him. The last time she fell asleep, she'd gone out like a light.

Not wanting his visitors to catch her looking so disheveled, she headed toward the bathroom, passing Chance in the hall.

"Morning, Hollywood."

"Morning," she grumbled, automatically glancing

at the dressing on his wound. "Somebody's at the door."

"I'm on my way to get it."

Kelly nodded and hurried on past him. He looked fresh and crisp in a pair of jeans, Western shirt with a thermal undershirt, boots and Stetson.

She, in turn, probably looked like a hag. She hadn't even brought a toothbrush.

In the bathroom, she rinsed her face and mouth, straightened her clothes and used Chance's brush on her hair.

Through the door, she heard voices— Eden and Stony had evidently dropped off the girls. She'd called the Strattons last night to let them know she was at Chance's place in case they needed to get in touch and couldn't reach her at the boardinghouse.

Kelly looked at her watch and frowned. It was early, and all sorts of reasons for them bringing the children home so soon flashed through her mind. Had the girls misbehaved?

And then the guilt set in. Eden had a darling three-month-old girl to take care of, as well as six-year-old Nikki. Kelly should have insisted on picking up the kids rather Eden disrupting her routine.

By the time Kelly got back to the living room, Eden and Stony were gone, and Chance was headed toward the door, Jessica and Kimmy's hands held in his.

Jessica spotted her and tugged Chance to a halt.

"Hi, Mommy. Kimmy missed you so we came home early."

Kelly crossed the room, knelt in front of her daughters and kissed each on the forehead. "I missed you

both, too." She had an idea Jessica had gotten homesick, too, but didn't push the issue. Despite their ea-
gerness for an overnight adventure, she should have
anticipated some separation anxiety.

"We're off to the barn to check the horses,"
Chance said. "Care to join us?"

She stood. "Brave man. You're going to take another chance on flying hooves?"

"Stony trains all my horses. They're much better
behaved than those donkeys. Bomb-proof, every one
of them."

"If you say so. I need coffee. Desperately. Then I'll
be out." If she could talk herself into braving the cold.
With just the front door open, the wind whipped in,
freezing her to the bone. It didn't seem to faze Chance
or the girls. Bundles of energy, all three of them.

And for children who claimed to miss her, they sure
scooted out the door in a hurry. Chance, also, seemed
fine, making her wonder why she'd felt such a strong
need to watch over him. Was it more than just medical
concern?

There was something about this man that drew her.

And that simply wasn't acceptable.

She wandered into his kitchen. It looked different
with sunlight streaming through the big window over
the sink, rather than the muted lighting of incandescent
bulbs she'd seen it in last night. The hardwood floors
were scuffed but lovingly maintained. The room had
a homey feel with lots of oak, ceramic tile and older
appliances, which probably functioned just fine despite
their age.

A half-full pot of coffee sat on the warmer and she poured a cup.

Sipping, she nearly spilled the hot brew down the front of her sweater when an older woman bustled into the kitchen.

"Oh, I startled you. I am Maria. I do the cooking and cleaning for the doctor."

"Hi, Maria." Kelly wiped coffee off her chin and looked around for a napkin. "I'm Kelly, Chance's…" What? Was she still his medical assistant? "I work with Chance."

"Oh, I know. The man has been talking of nothing else since you and the *niñas* came to town."

"He has?"

"Yes, and I can see why. *Muy bonita.*"

"Um, thank you." Kelly's Spanish wasn't great, but she knew enough to get by. And frankly, it had been a very long time since someone had told her she was pretty. She thought of herself as a doctor, competent, steady, no-nonsense—and always tired.

When had she stopped thinking of herself as a woman?

A long time ago.

But she knew the exact moment she'd begun to notice the oversight. The minute she'd laid eyes on Dr. Chance Hammond.

And darn it, this line of thinking wasn't going to get her anywhere. Best to let it go.

"Can I fix you some breakfast?" Maria asked.

"No. I'm fine with just coffee. Chance had a bit of an accident with a donkey last night, and I stayed to keep an eye on him.'' A subject she was going to discuss with him right away.

"Yes, I heard. It is wonderful news that you are a doctor. Our Chance works much too hard these days. He could use the help.''

She doubted this small town had much use for an orthopedic specialist. "Who told you I was a doctor?''

"Dr. Chance did, of course. I was fussing over his injury this morning, and he assured me he had been seen by the best doctor.''

This morning? Kelly nearly groaned. Had Chance and Maria been tiptoeing through the living room as she'd slept on the couch?

"Yes, well…I think I'd better go find him and make sure my daughters aren't talking his ear off.''

Maria laid a hand on Kelly's arm. "The little one, your Kimmy. She will get better. You wait and see.''

Kelly felt a lump form in her throat. The compassion was genuine. Lord, did everybody in town know her business?

Living in a small town was like being in a fishbowl.

But it was different than the media attention she'd suffered in California. Instead of chafing against strangers knowing her business, her heartaches, it felt right that these people knew.

They weren't out to exploit her or her children. They were simply standing in the wings waiting to offer whatever they had, whatever she needed.

"Thank you, Maria. I'm counting on it.''

IN THE BARN, Jessica was chattering like a magpie, asking questions and hardly waiting for Chance to answer. Even Kimberly was more animated than usual, having found a friendly border collie who was intent on licking her clean.

With her chubby arms around the dog's neck, her cheek laid on his fur, she reminded Kelly of the jubilant child she had once been—before tragedy had sent her inside herself.

Watching the patience Chance displayed with her daughters, she felt her heart soften. But not too much.

"I could have sworn you told me you had no one to keep an eye on you," she said.

Chance turned and grinned at her, leaning his weight on a huge rake. "Ah, you've met Maria."

"Yes. The woman who takes care of you."

"That's only during the day. She doesn't stay around to watch me sleep and make sure I wake up."

"But she would if you asked."

He shrugged. "I've never had the occasion to ask."

"Don't get many concussions, huh?" Why in the world couldn't this man have been the stereotypical old country doctor? Ancient and gray-haired? Why did he have to be so darn sexy?

"Nope, not since I was a kid. Besides, I like having the best watch over me."

"Flattery won't get you anywhere."

"It's worth a try. Come meet the horses."

She moved toward the wooden stall, but kept a respectful distance. The horse who swung its head around to get a look at her was tall with a gleaming chestnut coat, and a black tail and mane.

Kelly automatically took a step back and bumped into Chance.

He gazed down at her from beneath the brim of his black hat. "Horses make you nervous?"

"A little. I haven't been around them since I was a girl—aside from the donkey last night."

"This is Peppermint and she's a sweetheart. Come here." He put his arm around her shoulders, guided her closer. "Step over here to her side so she can see you better. She can't get a good look if you stand directly in front of her." With his hand over hers, he guided it to the horse's cheek, then up between Peppermint's ears.

"Oh, she's so soft."

"Just like a lady should be." His voice went deep and intimate. "Warm and soft."

Kelly was tempted to stomp on his foot but resisted. The man was an innate flirt and that was all there was to it. No sense trying to get a leopard to change his spots.

Besides, the warmth of his body next to hers was welcome. Although the barn was heated, Kelly was still cold.

She slipped her hand from beneath his and stepped away. "Well, this lady's freezing her butt off. I've never been in zero-degree weather, much less ten degrees below."

He chuckled. "Takes some getting used to." He studied her for several minutes. "I'm curious about something."

"What's that?"

"From what I gleaned last night of your marital situation and you and your husband's profession, I'm assuming your finances are healthy. So why'd you come to work for me?''

''I needed a break from the responsibilities of my own practice, more time to spend with the girls.''

''But clerical duties? You haven't been doctoring until last night.''

She glanced at the neat row of stalls, the stream of light coming through the windows, catching dust motes in the air. ''I didn't want to. I was happy just being in the medical environment. And you're only half-right about the finances.'' She glanced at Jessica and Kimberly, making sure they were occupied and not overhearing the conversation. The border collie and an old barn cat were doing a great job of keeping them entertained.

''Steve made a name for himself by taking years and inches off some of Hollywood's biggest stars. And he charged a pretty penny to do the glamorizing. But he also liked to gamble. He was what they call a high roller in Las Vegas. He placed big bets and he lost big. That was another nasty little secret I found out about after the funeral. Despite his debts, he never altered his lifestyle. He lived fast and lavishly.''

''So your money was squandered away, too?''

''Only a portion of it. My mother taught me that a woman should always have her own funds. In her day, they called it mad money, extra cash to get you home if a date went sour, a little stash that you could get your hands on in a hurry if you needed it. So I always kept part of my income separate from the household accounts. I'm far from bankrupt, but I'm also far from retiring.''

"Your mother sounds like a smart lady."

"She was."

"You lost her?"

"Two years ago to cancer."

"I'm sorry."

"Thanks. So, anyway, now you have most of my life history."

"I doubt we've even scratched the surface."

He brushed his knuckles tenderly over her cheek, and Kelly went absolutely still.

She didn't know what to say, didn't know if she could make a sound anyway. The barest touch of his fingers was mesmerizing.

His hands were wide and strong. A doctor's hands. A man's hands. They could heal or soothe or arouse.

And she was *not* going to trip off into la la land and fantasize about Chance Hammond's hands or their many skills.

She cleared her throat, then reached out on her own to stroke Peppermint's silky face.

Chance leaned a shoulder against the stall door and gave her space.

"How long are you planning to stay?"

"In Shotgun Ridge?" She glanced at Kimberly and Jessica. "Until the end of the year," she said softly. "Kimmy was like an empty shell before we came here. A tiny puppet who went through the motions. She's showing more life now. Look at her," she whispered. "She's smiling and playing with your dog like a normal little girl."

A normal little girl who still didn't speak.

The heartache and guilt were constant. Kelly felt the

emotions well up, tried like mad to swallow them back, tried to focus on the rough grain of wood, the swirl of a knot in the pine divider between stalls.

"Hey, Hollywood," Chance said gently, swiping a thumb beneath her eye. "It'll be fine. She'll come around."

"God, I hope so. I want to fix her, you know? I should be able to. I'm a doctor. I'm her mother. But I can't do it and it's tearing me up inside. My fancy medical degree doesn't mean squat in Kimberly's case."

"Kelly—"

"I have no idea what she thinks. Does she blame me? Does she blame herself? How much did she actually see? And how much did she actually understand? So many questions I just can't answer."

"Did you try a child psychologist?"

"Yes. No results. She doesn't act out like most four-year-olds, doesn't throw tantrums or giggle with joy. Something's locked inside, frozen, you know?"

He nodded, then shook his head because he *didn't* know. "I wish I had some answers."

"Your animals seem to be having an impact on both the girls. The old cat at Mildred and Opal's is so prissy she hardly ever lets the kids catch her."

"Miss Lucille," Chance said with a grin. "That's one ornery cat."

"Yes, and she's really going to get her nose out of joint in a few weeks. Mildred and Opal are expecting a full house for the holidays."

"Who's coming in?"

"Extended families is what I heard—Eden's and

Dora's for sure, and there's a plot brewing to get Emily's mother and stepfather here.''

"That would be great. Emily really wants her mom to come around and be a grandmother to those twins.''

"Well, holidays have a way of making families soften. Maybe it'll happen. In the meantime, though, you wouldn't happen to know of a place for rent around here, would you?''

"Surely the widows aren't going to ask you to leave. I happen to know that every single one of my buddies have homes big enough for the in-laws. You shouldn't have to—''

"No," Kelly interrupted. "The sisters would never ask me to leave. And though there's plenty of room at the Callahans' and Strattons', some of the family evidently want to stay in town. They've done it in years past and it's become a tradition.''

"And you're not keen on crowds, right?''

"It's not that, really. I would like to get something with a little more privacy though, a place where my kids have more room to play. In fact, after seeing the girls with your animals, I might get them a pet for Christmas, maybe one for each of them.''

"Animals have been known to work wonders when medicine and science hit a brick wall.''

"Seems there's merit there.'' She did a double take, then laughed when she saw a chicken come into the barn, strutting as if it owned the place. The minute Jessica spotted it, she gave chase.

Feathers ruffled, the chicken ran for all it was worth.

"Jess, don't chase the chicken,'' Kelly called.

Jessica skidded to a halt and obeyed, but the dog

didn't. The chicken squawked and the dog barked, apparently showing off for his audience.

"You've got quite a farm here."

Chance chuckled. "There are people who still pay me in eggs, so you wouldn't think I'd need my own laying hens. But somebody actually paid me with the chickens, and I ended up keeping them. The cat was a stray, and I think there are a couple more around here. The dog and horses, I chose. Not really a farm."

"Scout!" Jessica hollered sweetly. "Mommy said not to chase the chicken. There's a good puppy. Come here now, sweetie." She lavished praise and kisses on the dog when it panted happily at her feet. Ears perked, tongue lolling, the dog looked back and forth from Jessica to Kimberly, then gave each little girl a lick.

Kelly felt her heart stand still as she saw the tiny dimples peek out of Kimberly's cheeks.

Come on, baby. Let it out. Giggle for all you're worth.

"It's right there just below the surface," Chance said close to Kelly's ear.

She nodded and turned to him. He stood so close, looking down at her. Lord, she'd never known a man in a cowboy hat could look so sexy. She'd definitely been cooped up in a doctor's office and hospital far too long.

"I gave staying in town a trial run, was hoping that Mildred and Opal's sweetness—or their antics—would spark something in Kimmy. It didn't, so maybe this is my next step. Renting something else for a while. Got any suggestions?"

"Actually I do. Why don't you move in with me?"

They'd had a twenty-minute conversation, and the sounds of horses, kids and animals had masked their words. Wouldn't you know there'd be a lull in the noise at the precise moment he uttered those seven words.

She glanced at Kimberly and Jessica. Both girls had gone still, watching her, all ears.

"I don't think—"

"It's a big place, Kelly, with only me and Maria rattling around. Maria can watch the girls while you're at work. The bedrooms are split, with suites at both ends of the house. You could probably go for days without seeing me if you wanted. We've got animals and wide open spaces, and we're still close to town. What do you say?"

"Yes!" Jessica shrieked, hopping up and down, inciting Scout into a barking fit. "Yes, Mommy! Please, please, please!"

Through a forced smile, Kelly muttered, "You did that on purpose. Just like with the sleigh."

He placed a hand over his heart, his expression one of complete innocence.

He was about as innocent as a fox in a henhouse. He'd raised his voice ever so slightly so the girls would hear and add their argument, yea or nay.

Actually it wasn't really so underhanded, when she thought about it. The pendulum could have swung in the other direction. He'd actually given the girls a chance to voice an objection. If they didn't like the idea, then Kelly would have known it right off.

"Kimmy?" she asked.

The tiny girl bobbed her head, her eyes filled with entreaty and hope.

It was that spark of hope that made up Kelly's mind.

She desperately wanted her daughter to heal, and she'd do anything to see that happen. Even living on a ranch with the town's sexy single doctor.

Chapter Four

It only took one load in Chance's truck to get Kelly and her daughters' clothes and a few prized toys moved out to his ranch.

They were traveling pretty light, reminding him that the move to Shotgun Ridge was temporary. A test. A last-ditch effort of a mother who'd exhausted most other avenues and didn't know where to turn next.

Chance knew Kelly wasn't here for the long haul and wondered if he was setting himself up for a fall by tangling himself in her life this way.

The problem was, he couldn't do anything else. He was drawn to this woman and her little girls.

Perhaps it was arrogant to think, or hope, that he could somehow heal these three when others had tried and failed. But he had to give it a shot.

The sound of feminine voices in his home—a sexy alto and childish sopranos—took a little getting used to.

He stopped by the room Jessica and Kimmy had insisted on sharing. Although he had plenty of bedrooms for each girl to have her own, they'd wanted to stay together. He imagined it had to do with the fear of ''monsters'' that lurked inside young hearts.

Well, there were no monsters beneath the mahogany double bed or anywhere else in the house, and he hoped to make sure everyone learned that.

''Man alive, how many clothes do you ladies have?''

Kelly turned, hanger in her hand, a child's pink sweater draped over it. Jessica and Kimmy were stuffing things willy-nilly into drawers.

''We've added to our wardrobe since we've been here,'' Kelly said. ''We weren't prepared for the weather.''

''Mmm. Best way to get used to it is go out in it.''

''I'd opt for a fire and a cup of something hot.''

He grinned and winked. ''Later. Right now we've got a million things to do.''

''Besides hanging up all these clothes?''

''That's boring stuff.''

Obviously sensing an adventure, Jessica and Kimberly abandoned their unpacking chore and shoved the dresser drawer closed. The sleeve of some bunny pajamas and a stray sock got caught in the rush and hung down the front of the cherry-wood dresser like Christmas stockings waiting for Santa to fill with gifts.

''What do we gotta do?'' Jessica asked.

''First, we need to get a Christmas tree. And maybe we should dash off a quick note to Santa to let him know where you are.''

Jessica obviously hadn't thought about that and looked worried. Chance couldn't tell if Kimmy was worried or not. His heart squeezed.

"Do you think he'll find us?" Jess asked.

"Of course. We'll write that letter, and I'll mail it to him on our way to the tree farm."

"What if it doesn't get to the North Pole in time?"

"Ah, not to worry, little one. The post office does overnight express delivery. He'll get it."

"Okay! Come on, Kimmy. We gotta write a note. Mommy, do you got paper? It should be pretty." Jessica looked at Chance. "Do you got stickers? Kimmy likes the snowmans and I like angels."

Chance frowned. "Uh, I don't think I have stickers."

"Do you have a computer here?" Kelly asked.

"Yes, in the study."

"If you don't mind her messing with it, Jessica can look and see if you have a graphics program loaded on it."

"You know how to work the computer?" he asked Jessica.

She gave him a look that suggested he'd asked an incredibly stupid question. "'Course. Every girl learns these things," she said, sounding more like a Southern belle lecturing on etiquette than a six-year-old child.

He ruffled her hair, then cupped Kimmy's cheeks to include her. "And I suppose you know computers, too? Well, of course you do," he said before she could nod or break his heart by not answering on her own. "Silly me. Let's go fire that sucker up and design a map for Santa Claus. Imagine how embarrassed he'd be if he went to the wrong house, then had to search the universe looking for Jessica and Kimberly Anderson. It'd throw off his schedule something fierce."

He looked up at Kelly, caught the yearning in her eyes, the ache and uncertainty of a mother, and the reserved joy, too. She loved these girls to distraction. That was clear.

"Coming, Hollywood?"

She gave him a smile that tugged at his heart and made his libido sing. How could one woman touch him and excite him so thoroughly at once?

"Yes. I'm coming. I did quite well in English. You might need my input on sentence structure or something."

He affected a scandalized expression. "Santa doesn't critique his mail!"

Jessica giggled. "Come on, Kimmy. But don't step on Marcy's dress." Kimmy took a huge sideways step as though skirting someone and followed Jessica through the door.

Chance looked at Kelly. "Marcy?"

"Her imaginary angel."

"Oh." He glanced around the room, then felt ridiculous. Especially when Kelly laughed. "Well," he said, defending himself, "you never know."

"Don't you start, too."

"Hey, imagination's healthy." And his own was glowing with good health.

But right now, he needed to get his mind off his sexy boarder and focus on his plan.

To show Kelly Anderson and her girls the best Christmas they'd ever had.

He couldn't put a bandage on or stitch up the pain and trauma this family had gone through, but in this case, maybe the treatment course had less to do with medical skill and more to do with the miracle of the season and a loving town.

He had both at his disposal and vowed to used them shamelessly.

KELLY WAS FREEZING half to death. In theory, a white Christmas with snow on the ground and crisp, pine-scented air carrying strains of familiar carols was a wonderful image. In reality, it was bone-rattling, spine-shivering discomfort.

She put her hands in her coat pockets and tried to think warm thoughts. They'd been traipsing through the snow-covered tree lot looking for the ''perfect'' Christmas tree for at least forty-five minutes, and her feet felt like blocks of ice.

Honestly. They all looked pretty much the same to Kelly—snow-dusted, crooked branches, most of them stretching higher than the top of Chance's Stetson. Your basic everyday Christmas tree.

But Jessica wasn't yet satisfied and Chance was indulging her. Her precocious daughter insisted she'd know the perfect tree because it would talk to her.

Kelly wished one of the firs would hurry up and speak because she was freezing her buns off.

She glanced down at Kimberly, who was sticking close, probably not wanting her mom to feel left out since Jess and Chance had paired up like a couple of happy elves. ''You warm enough, sweetie?''

Kimmy nodded and reached out to touch one of the trees with her mitten-covered hands.

''This one looks nice,'' Chance commented from behind them. ''What do you think, Jess?''

Kelly glanced back and watched as Jessica and Chance shook the branches of a Douglas fir.

"Hi, Miss Tree," Jessica said. "You're very pretty. You wanna go home with me?"

"We have a nice warm house and a very tall ceiling for you to spread your branches in," Chance added.

A smile tugged at Kelly's lips, despite the fact that her face was nearly numb. Jessica and Chance were openly conversing with the trees. She felt a twinge of motherly worry that her daughter was talking to too many imaginary things lately.

She was startled into immobility when a tree actually talked back.

"No! Not her! Take me, instead!" sang a masculine voice.

"No, don't listen to him. Take me, I'm prettier!"

"What in the world?" Kelly murmured, astonished. It sounded as though the voice was actually coming from the trees—and Chance's lips weren't moving. She'd checked.

In fact, he looked a little jolted himself.

It's the season for miracles.

Kelly was rational enough, however, to know the trees weren't talking. Someone was behind them throwing his voice.

But Jessica didn't know that and jumped right into the debate without missing a beat, absolutely delighted. The intricacies of a child's mind continually amazed Kelly.

"Are you a boy or a girl tree?" Jessica asked. Her face was earnest, as though talking to bushy firs was an everyday occurrence. Blond hair spiked out beneath her red knit stocking cap, and Kelly noticed that her coat was unbuttoned again.

"I'm the girl. Miss Tree at your service, sweetheart." The high singsong voice came from the tree Jessica had originally been speaking to.

"And I'm the boy." This was said in a deep baritone from the branches of the tree on the left.

Shifting slightly, Kelly caught a glimpse of leather gloves manipulating one of the branches as though the tree was waving and pleading for purchase.

The preacher. She should have guessed.

Jessica folded her arms and gave serious consideration to both trees. "Which one do you like, Chance?"

"Well, I'm kind of partial to the boy tree since I'm a bit outnumbered in a house full of girls."

"Oh, horrors," the tree sang. "Never ask a man these questions. Let's get Kimmy's vote."

"Good idea," Chance said, turning and holding his hand out for Kimberly. "Come tell us which one you like best."

"Foul!" cried the male tree.

Kimmy's eyes widened, as did Jessica's. Kelly figured they'd probably pick the one on the left—the boy—because they'd feel sorry for it. Chance obviously thought the same thing.

"Hey, that's not fair." He spoke to the objecting tree, and Kelly nearly laughed. "The whole family has a say in this, so behave yourself."

"Kimmy doesn't talk," Jessica told the tree.

"That's okay," the tree responded in a kindly voice—the girl tree this time. "Trees don't talk, either."

"But you do."

"Only until someone buys me and takes me home. I talk when the time is right, when the perfect family happens along."

Smart move, Kelly thought. The preacher had gently given Kimmy permission to speak if she was ready, and offered an explanation why the tree wouldn't talk back once they got it home.

Chance took Kimmy's hand, then his gaze locked onto Kelly's. "You, too, Hollywood. Come help out here."

What woman wouldn't be drawn by the searing intensity of Chance Hammond's single powerful look?

His eyes held her like a caress, both sexy and full of fun. It was simply beyond her power to resist him at that moment, and she moved to his side.

As though they'd been a couple for years, he slung an arm around her shoulders, drawing her against his warmth.

The whole family has a say in this.

The four of them standing there as a group did indeed feel like a family. And that was dangerous.

It gave the girls false hope.

Because they *weren't* a foursome. It was just the three of them—Kelly, Jessica and Kimmy. And it needed to stay that way. Jess and Kimmy had been through enough changes lately.

But the hopeful expression on her daughters' faces kept Kelly right where she was, snuggled—a bit stiffly—against Chance's side.

The talking trees were drawing a crowd, and Kelly

didn't know whether to laugh, apologize or join in the lunacy.

"Well, now, looks to me like somebody found their perfect tree, you bet." Ozzie Peyton, clad in a heavy coat, wool scarf and gloves, nodded his head. "My Vanessa always said when it's the right tree, it'll let you know it. Spent a good many Christmases walkin' my legs off waiting for one to open up and give the word, you bet."

"If somebody doesn't hurry up and make a decision, I'll be needing treatment for hypothermia," she muttered, trying to keep her teeth from chattering.

Chance glanced down at her and winked. "Okay, it's between Mr. Tree and Miss Tree. What do you say, girls?"

Jessica conferred with Kimberly, then looked up at Chance. "Kimmy doesn't want them to be sad. Could we get them both?"

"Jess—"

Chance squeezed Kelly's shoulder. "Now, why didn't I think of that? One for the house and one for the clinic. Perfect."

"Been sayin' that ourselves for a while now," Ozzie murmured. "'Bout time somebody started to pay attention." His twinkling blue gaze shifting to his friends, who stood behind him, then back to Kelly and the girls.

Kelly had an idea his statement had nothing to do with Christmas trees and everything to do with the fact that she and Chance looked as though they had something cozy and intimate going on between them.

THEY DROPPED OFF one of the trees at the clinic on their way home—the boy tree. There had been some debate over which one it was since the branches were no longer talking, and this time it was the angel who'd helped with the decision.

Chance hadn't batted an eye when Jessica claimed the angel was speaking to her. In fact, he'd had to apologize for nearly knocking Marcy's wings askew when he'd muscled the Christmas tree through the door, and he'd done so with such seriousness everyone had collapsed into a fit of giggles.

Kelly couldn't remember a time when she'd been so relaxed, had so much fun. Looked forward to whatever would come next.

She'd been so caught up in planning her life, running on schedules, knowing what needed to be done each minute of the day that she hadn't realized everything she'd missed. The laughter, the mischief in her daughter's eyes, the silliness.

Even when she'd been home, she'd been thinking about work. How many times had she said, "Uh-huh," yet never even heard what her children had said? Why hadn't she paid better attention?

And why hadn't she ever made this big of a fuss over Christmas?

Chance was thoroughly into the spirit, as much a kid as Jessica and Kimberly. It was hard not to get swept into the enthusiasm.

And there was plenty of it to go around. Decorating a tree in Montana was an involved process. They didn't simply dive into boxes of ornaments or pull garland out of a package and drape it prettily on the branches.

Instead, they sat at the kitchen table, drinking spiced cider and cocoa, stringing popcorn and cranberries on silk medical thread—the same kind she'd used to stitch up Chance's head.

Chance was wielding the needle, and the girls had formed an assembly line. They were in charge of handing him the food stuff, then moving the goodies along the thread like red and white beads on a gaudy necklace.

Kelly was supervising and unrolling the silk line. And trying her best to keep up with the jumble of confusing, conflicting emotions that raced through her as she watched her daughters respond to Chance's attention.

"I saw that," Chance said when Jessica poked a piece of popcorn into her mouth. The little girl giggled.

He scooped up a handful and tossed it in the air toward each girl's mouth. "Open up."

Like fish bobbing for food at the surface of an aquarium tank, they both tilted their heads back, trying to catch the fragrant kernels in their mouths. Popcorn littered the floor like confetti. Kelly's sense of organization objected and she wanted to reach over and sweep it up, but Scout got into the game, lapping up the stray pieces of corn. Kelly made herself relax and enjoy the silliness of the whole thing.

They strung and ate and sipped and laughed. It was the most fun she'd had in ages.

When Chance deemed the garland plenty long

enough to wind around the tree, he coiled it up, grabbed Kelly's hand and tugged her into the living room, leaving Jessica and Kimberly in the kitchen to make snowflakes. Kelly didn't know whether to laugh or object to his steamroller tactics.

"Who made you the boss of decorating?" she asked.

"I did." He grinned at her, clearly unrepentant and in his element. "Lights first."

The tree was so tall he had to use a ladder for the uppermost branches. "As your doctor, I'd like to point out yet again that you shouldn't be exerting yourself."

"This isn't exertion. It's tradition."

"Tradition can wait a few days. We don't have to decorate the tree tonight."

He gazed down at her from his perch. "Now I ask you. Who can leave an undecorated tree sitting in the living room all bare and forlorn-looking?"

"A man with a concussion?" she offered, hiding her smile. It was tough to try to pull rank when you couldn't keep a straight face. Though, she had to admit, in terms of doctoring, their rank was pretty much equal.

"I don't have a concussion. The critical time has passed and you know it. Get in the spirit, woman."

"Fine. But if you fall off that ladder, I'm not stitching you up."

"Bet you would."

She sighed. Of course she would. She was a doctor. It was her job. Never mind that when she'd seen Chance lying unconscious yesterday, even for only a few seconds, her reaction had been as a woman first and doctor second.

As he looped colored lights around the upper branches of the tree, Kelly helped out by holding the box and feeding more wire as he needed it. The ladder didn't look all that stable, and she had an urge to put a hand on his leg to steady him.

She resisted, knowing that if she touched him, even innocently, she'd want to do a whole lot more. The man was a god, six feet of fantasy-evoking masculinity. Jeans hugged his hips and long legs. He'd taken off his button-front shirt and wore a skin-tight thermal one tucked into the waistband of those sexy jeans. Muscles rippled beneath the heavy cotton material.

"Woolgathering, Hollywood?"

Her gaze snapped to his. That devilish smile sent her heart rate up another notch.

"I'd like to be gathering wool—and burrowing in it. I still feel like an icicle." She unrolled more of the lights and told herself to pay attention to the job at hand and stop drooling over her landlord.

"Why don't you go on over by the fire and thaw out?"

"We've been inside an hour. You'd think I'd be a puddle by now."

He raised a brow, took a step down the ladder. "Maybe I can do something about that."

She backed up as far as the string of lights would allow—which wasn't nearly far enough to avoid the deliberate brush of his body when he reached the bottom of the ladder.

"Don't start," she warned.

He grinned, moved impossibly closer. She could smell pine sap and crisp winter air on his skin, mingled with the sweet tangy scent of cider on his breath.

Good Lord, was he going to kiss her?

She wouldn't put it past him to be holding a sprig of mistletoe over her head. The man was devious. And so sexy every vital sign in her body had gone haywire.

His gaze slipped to her mouth. Just when she thought she'd die if he *didn't* kiss her, he stepped aside.

"I was talking about adding a log to the fire," he said. "What did you think I meant?"

He knew very well what she thought—that he was going to warm her and turn her into a puddle using his body and kisses. And darn it all, she ought to stop this right now, take herself out of the room and away from temptation, but she was still holding the box of lights, and the other end of the string was attached to the tree.

Plucking at the neck of her sweater, she realized that she wasn't cold anymore. In fact, she was burning up.

She didn't bother to tell him so. The man was too sure of himself for his own good. It wouldn't do to feed that ego. But oh, she wanted to.

And knew without a doubt that it would be a very bad idea. He was her landlord. He was a small-town doctor entrenched in this wonderful town.

She had a medical practice in California waiting for her return. And she didn't want to give her daughters the wrong impression.

She had no idea how they felt about her seeing another man. They might feel threatened by such a relationship, see it as a betrayal of their father. Or they might begin to hope...hope for a complete family.

In either case, she would be adding to the burdens they already shouldered, burdens that neither little girl would discuss. Jessica chattered constantly, but was flippant or changed the subject when Kelly tried to bring up the past, to probe for feelings. Kimberly had simply gone inside herself.

And until she found a way to heal her children, Kelly couldn't even think about herself. Chance brought out the womanly needs in her that had been long neglected, but she couldn't give in to those needs.

Too bad that sensible decision didn't stop the yearning.

Chance took the dangling string of lights from her hands, startling her. "Deep thoughts?"

"I suppose."

"I've been told I'm a very good listener."

Holding the box, she followed him as he circled the tree arranging lights on the branches. "Some of those thoughts were about you." Oh, damn. She hadn't meant to blurt that.

He paused and she nearly plowed into his back. "Now that's the kind of thing I like to hear."

"Don't get your hopes up, ace."

He sighed and resumed his task. "It's Christmastime. Give a guy a break."

"You're such a flirt."

He went still again, pinned her with a look that made her squirm. "I can be quite serious."

"Don't, okay?"

He watched her, patiently, curiously. Then he

glanced toward the kitchen door where the kids were safely out of earshot.

"Tell me something."

"What?"

"Did you love him?"

Kelly glanced down at the box of lights in her hands, cold now, with only a hint of the color that would glisten once they were plugged in. "Yes, I did. And I loved Candy, too. I don't know which betrayal hurt worse."

"I assume the friendship ended?"

Nodding, she handed him the last of the lights then set the box aside. "The girls don't understand, and I don't know how to explain it to them."

"Time and distance will help."

"But what about when I go back?"

He reached out and gently ran the back of his fingers over her cheek. She should have moved away, but the touch felt too good. She wanted to lean into him.

"Don't borrow trouble before it finds you," he said softly.

"That's just the problem. Trouble found us months ago. Maybe even years. And I was too damned blind and wrapped up in my work to notice."

"That was before. This is now. Take each day as it comes."

"Each day I feel more like a failure." The admission slipped out, stunning her, trapping her breath in her lungs. Her eyes stung like alcohol poured on a raw wound, but she wouldn't give in. Couldn't. She hadn't cried for herself in six months. She'd cried for her kids, but not herself. If she started now, she might never stop.

Chance bent his knees, bringing his face level with hers. "Look here, Hollywood."

With his hands on her shoulders, his eyes in her direct line of sight, she could do little else.

"You have not failed. It's not your fault that your husband didn't treasure what he had. It's not your fault that he died or that your little girl is temporarily trapped in silence."

"How do you know? You don't know me. You don't know what I was like."

"I want to."

She looked into his blue eyes, saw the seriousness, and the desire. He'd never hidden his emotions from her. But he hadn't pushed, either. This was a man a woman could trust. But she wasn't the woman for him.

"You're asking for more than I can give."

"Can give? Or *want* to give?"

"Does it matter?"

"I think it does."

She stepped back. "Don't make me regret moving in here." But she already did regret it. For selfish reasons. Because he made her yearn for more, and that scared her, made her want to run, made it difficult to remember her purpose. Her children.

She couldn't, however, regret the change that was taking place in her daughters.

She was caught in a quandary of conflict. The battle between the woman in her and the mother was so fierce it made her dizzy.

"Who takes care of you, Doc?" he asked quietly.

The question blindsided her, sent her emotions spinning even higher. Her throat ached and she had no idea why. "What are you talking about?"

"You know what I'm talking about. You've dedicated your life to taking care of other people, doctoring. Then you come here alone, isolating yourself, shouldering the sole responsibility for your family. Who's there for you?"

"I don't need anyone."

"Everyone needs someone." He brushed a strand of hair off her cheek. "Someone to talk to, to share a hug. Someone to help with the dishes or cook a meal. Someone to rub your feet after a long day or just hold you when you lose a patient or get overwhelmed. I'm going to take a wild guess that your husband didn't do that for you."

Before she could think better of it, she shook her head, admitting he was right on target.

"Well, let me tell you something. Out here in Montana, our mamas raise us to be cowboys and gentlemen. Taking care is part of us just like breathing."

"Chance—"

He put a finger over her lips. "No sense arguing. You can't ask a horse to change his coat. It's my nature to help out a friend in need."

"A friend."

"That's what we are to each other, aren't we?"

"I'd like to think so."

He smiled. "I know, it's difficult with all the other stuff that gets tangled up, too. You're probably finding it pretty hard to resist my charms."

He was so absurdly serious she burst out laughing. "You're so full of it, Hammond."

He stepped back and nodded. "Got you to laugh, though, didn't I?"

"You're sneaky."

"No." He paused, held her with his gaze. "I'm damned good."

Kelly's laughter ended on a groan of longing so shockingly blatant her face went red with embarrassment.

She closed her eyes. It had been too long since she'd had sex. That was all there was to it. Otherwise she wouldn't be putting a sexual connotation on every little thing he said.

Even though she imagined he *had* meant it in a sexual way, the maddening man would deny it for sure.

"Let's go see if the kids have those ornaments cut out," he said as though the sexual tension between them was a figment of her imagination.

She could've cheerfully hit him. He sashayed out of the room with a loose-hipped stride that made her heart pump and butterflies take wing in her stomach. He knew damned well that he'd gotten to her.

And because she was feeling petulant, she stuck her tongue out at his retreating back. The impulsive action astonished her so much she laughed. My Lord, Kelly Anderson, child prodigy who'd graduated from college at eighteen, had just done something totally spontaneous and ridiculous.

Chance glanced over his shoulder, brows raised in inquiry. She shook her head and motioned him into the kitchen. She didn't think he'd appreciate the irony.

Chapter Five

Jessica and Kimberly had crayons, construction paper and glitter scattered all over the kitchen table. Jessica was still hard at work on the snowflakes, but Kimmy had drawn a little girl and cut it out like a paper doll.

"Hey, this is really good," Chance said, examining the drawing. "This girl looks just like you. Is it?"

Kimmy nodded and Chance brushed a hand lightly over her blond hair, bringing another lump to Kelly's throat. He was a man who touched often, without thought or reciprocal expectations.

"I didn't know you were an artist. We'll have to hang this right at the front of the tree. In fact, I think we should all have our own ornament. Here." He handed Jessica and Kelly each a crayon. "Everybody has to draw themselves."

"I can't draw," Kelly said.

"Sure you can. Kimmy will help if you get stuck."

"*I* don't need help," Jessica said indignantly, just in case he was suggesting that her artistic talents weren't equal to her little sister's.

"I can see that. You did a fine job on the snowflakes. Two talented girls among us. It's your mom I'm worried about.''

He prodded and shamed until Kelly was forced to join in. Then he bent his head to his own task, sketching and shading, reaching for different-colored crayons, concentrating as though he was an architect drawing blueprints. Or the son of a famous artist.

Kelly could hardly make any headway with her own assignment because she kept looking over at what he was doing.

''No fair copying.''

''I'm not copying.'' But she'd like to. Her own drawing attempt was pitiful and embarrassing.

Chance's was practically a portrait. He'd drawn the outline of a cowboy complete with boots and hat, carefully cut it out, then sketched a stethoscope around the neck, instead of the traditional bandanna.

What did she expect? The man had a healthy dose of creativity in his genes. She, on the other hand, had been carving cadavers when other kids her age were in art class. Still, how difficult was it to make an ornament?

Jessica had drawn herself holding a dog with pointy ears. Kimmy noticed and added a pet to her own ornament—a wild-eyed cat with stringy whiskers and a tail as fat as its body.

Kelly had only gotten as far as cutting out the female image. And a pitiful one at that. She could cut open a human body and stitch it back up with skill that hardly left a scar—an artistic feat she was quite proud of—but she couldn't draw a decent paper doll.

''Let's see,'' Chance said. He gazed at Jessica's girl

ornament and nodded. "Oh, good. You got Scout in there. He'd have had his feelings hurt if we didn't include him. And Kimmy's got—" he studied the drawing "—Miss Lucille? Naw, that old cat's too prissy. I bet this one's Fluff. I can tell by the bushy tail."

A pleased expression replaced the usual emptiness and unresponsiveness of Kimmy's features, making Kelly's heart ache in both joy and sorrow.

How much emotion was trapped inside her daughter? How many times had she been misunderstood because her words were unable to find a voice? The frustration of not being able to communicate was more than likely harder on Kimmy than on the rest of them.

Kelly couldn't imagine how her little girl felt. Alone? Scared?

Reaching over, she scooped Kimmy off the chair and held her daughter close to her heart. She smelled of crayons and glue and baby shampoo. Kelly just wanted to hug her into talking, wanted to kiss it and make it better.

Like her own mother had done countless times.

A wave of sadness swept her, so strong she nearly wept with it. Oh, God, she longed for her mom.

The sadness sneaked up on her at odd moments, an emptiness that would never go away. Oh, it would ease, tuck itself away beneath the trials of everyday living, but it would always be there ready to surface when a smell or a word or a touch sparked a memory. Like now.

Mom had always known how to make things better. Even though Kelly was the doctor in the family, she'd

still called her mother for advice. She longed to pick
up the phone now, to hear her mother's sweet voice,
to rest in the absolute confidence she'd always felt
when her mother told her everything would be all
right.

*Tell me how to fix my little girl, Mom. Tell me it'll
be all right.*

Kimberly squirmed and Kelly realized she was
squeezing her daughter too hard. She loosened her
hold and Kimmy slid off her lap, her little tennis shoes
making a soft plopping noise on the hardwood floor.

What kind of a mother was she? She hadn't held
on hard enough when she should have, hadn't protected them. And now, she had an idea she was holding on *too* hard.

"Ready, Kel?" Chance said, standing with Jessica
and Kimberly close by his side. His gaze was filled
with compassion...and something else. He had no way
of knowing what she was thinking, but he was a man
who noticed nuances. Sometimes that was all a doctor
had to go on—mannerisms, the way patients acted
rather than what they said.

She wasn't his patient. But he was a perceptive man.

A protective man.

Who takes care of you, Doc?

It would be very easy to lean on him, to let him
share her burdens. It was going to be a fierce battle to
keep from doing just that.

KELLY WASN'T HAVING any luck falling asleep. The
queen-size bed was comfortable enough, but the atmosphere was still new and unfamiliar. Shadows played

over the walls, reflecting in the dresser mirror. Wind batted the windows like a stranger asking to come in.

The kids were in their own bed, a spacious double across the hall, and Chance had gone out on a house call. A woman had phoned complaining of chest pains.

House calls. Being here was like stepping back into another era. Everything was so different. Right down to the Christmas tree they'd decorated that evening.

There had been laughter and bickering and sensuality.

The sensuality part was probably why she was still wide awake.

They'd hung all the ornaments on the tree, most of them homemade. Then Kelly had turned and picked up the angel. Without permission or warning, Chance had lifted her as though she weighed no more than Kimberly and held her aloft to position it on the tree-top.

It was the tactile memory of her back taking that slow erotic slide down the front of his body that kept replaying in her mind, though.

"Stop it, Kelly." She pulled the quilt higher, clutching it under her chin to keep the chill air out, focusing her mind on the safer aspects of the tree. When they'd finished, she'd suffered a moment of dismay at the haphazard way the handmade ornaments were hung. It looked a little crazy, like a child's tree. A far cry from the color-coordinated, strategically placed, shiny golds and reds she usually had.

Yet the girls had never been this excited about their elegantly appointed California tree. Tonight their faces had glowed with happiness. Even Kimmy's. And they'd made Kelly promise that every year from now on they'd string popcorn and cranberries and have a tree exactly like this one.

Traditions. They were building more of them with Chance in a single week than she had with Steve in eight years. Sleigh rides, live nativity scenes, popcorn garlands—what next?

A loud crash had her sitting straight up in bed, adrenaline pouring through her system. She strained her ears, trying to listen past the pounding of her heart.

This was her first night living on Chance's ranch, and because it was all so unfamiliar, she felt vulnerable. Last night had been different. She'd slept on the couch, merely a visitor. Chance had been home, and her children had been safe at Eden and Stony's.

Now if something went bump in the night, it was up to her to investigate. Oh, God, she didn't want to. Chance had taken the dog with him, so she couldn't count on ferocious barking and snarling to scare off a potential prowler.

Scared half out of her mind and annoyed with herself because of it, Kelly slipped out of bed, put on her fleecy robe and slippers, and looked out the window.

Chance was still gone. If he'd come home, she'd have heard his truck or seen his headlights flash in her bedroom window.

She jumped when she heard the noise again. It sounded like someone was trying to come in the back door. Quickly she made her way across the hall to check on the girls. They were both asleep.

She wasn't the bravest person on the planet, but she knew she had to investigate the noise. If someone was outside, she needed to call the sheriff, protect her kids. But she didn't want to drag the deputies out to Chance's house on a wild-goose chase.

Her nerves jumped and her fingers tingled. Adrenaline still had her heart thumping in her chest. Well, damn it, it was spooky being in an unfamiliar house, out here all alone with just her girls. She was used to the boardinghouse, and before that, having neighbors only six feet away—clearly within calling distance.

Talk about a fish out of water—that was exactly how she felt.

She crept into the living room, where the fire was nothing more than orange embers in the grate. The tree stood in the corner like a menacing shadow. Instead of twinkling lights, construction-paper ornaments glowed white against the dark green. Watching her.

Oh, for heaven's sake. She was working herself into a state.

The sound came again. Closer. Heart thundering, she stood on the hearth, retrieved the key hidden in an urn Chance had pointed out to her earlier, and unlocked the shotgun rack that hung high over the fireplace mantel. She had no idea if the weapon was loaded, had only a marginal idea of how to fire it— which she was *not* going to do. But she could use it to scare someone off. Or to hit them over the head.

Armed with a mother's protective instincts, self-preservation and not a speck of confidence, she flipped on the porch light outside the back door and peered through the window, half expecting to see a face staring back at her. She'd have died on the spot if there had been.

There was no movement and no noise. She ought to just go back to bed. But she'd come this far. She'd never rest if she didn't satisfy herself that all was well.

Certain that she was overreacting and being ridiculous, she eased open the back door. A blast of frigid air stung her cheeks, swirled beneath the collar of her robe.

She stepped outside, gun pointed, one finger on the trigger. A button shifted beneath her thumb, but since the gun didn't do anything ominous, she didn't bother to look down.

A scratching noise had her whirling around.

She didn't know who was more scared. Her or the raccoon that looked up at her. Her hands trembled and her arms shook with the weight of the shotgun.

"For heaven's sa—"

The next several seconds happened too fast for Kelly to process. A horribly ugly animal darted out from behind the trash cans, charging right for her. Not the raccoon, but another creature.

She slammed her eyes shut. *Oh God, oh God, oh God...*

Reflexively, accidentally, she squeezed the trigger and scared herself silly when the shotgun unexpectedly blasted fire and kicked hard against her shoulder.

Oh, dear Lord. Had she hit it? She wanted to open her eyes and look, but she was afraid of what she'd see. A poor animal blown to smithereens or one charging at her with its teeth bared? In either case, she took her hand completely away from the trigger, eliminating the chance of another accidental firing.

"Hey there, Annie Oakley."

Kelly screamed and whirled around.

Chance held up his hands, even though the shotgun was pointing toward the ground. "Do me a favor, babe, and press that little Safety button under your thumb."

"That's what got me in trouble in the first place." Her hands were shaking so badly it took a moment to locate the switch thing. "Damn it, Chance. You scared me half to death."

"Scared that possum more, I suspect."

"A possum? Did I hurt it?"

"Nope. Killed the trash can, though. A shame. I was kind of partial to that one."

"The…?" Sure enough, the plastic trash barrel had a huge hole ripped in its side.

Chance stood in the moonlight, hat cocked back on his head, shoulder resting on the porch post, amusement dancing in his sexy-as-sin blue eyes. She had a very real and unladylike urge to scream again.

She'd never live this down, she was sure of it.

"I'll buy you a new one." Her tone was surly. There was no help for it. She was mortified and shaken to the core. And freezing her butt off. Again! The timing of her visit to Montana was off by a good six months—unless they never had a summer in this part of the country.

"Here." She shoved the shotgun into his hands and marched back into the house with as much dignity as she could muster.

Chance watched her go, then followed her inside. She was standing in front of the fireplace, where the dying embers put out hardly any warmth.

He shifted her to the side and decided against grinning when he saw the look on her face. He had sisters, so he was pretty good at reading a woman's mood.

This one was contemplating murder.

"I'll just put this away." He'd already cracked the barrel and unloaded the gun, so now he lifted it back on the rack above the mantel and relocked the safety clamps that held it in place.

"You think I'm an idiot, don't you."

"No. You ever shot a gun before?"

"The answer to that ought to be fairly obvious. And I didn't intentionally shoot that one."

"Mmm." His lip was going to bleed if he kept biting it. "I'll take you out and give you some pointers."

"Wait until spring and I might take you up on it." Summer would be better.

He tossed a log on the fire, looked at her. Would she still be here come spring? Could he convince her to stay? Could he compete with her world and her medical practice waiting for her in California? He doubted it. And for that reason alone, he ought to guard his heart, keep his distance.

Trouble was, he didn't often do things that were all that good for him. Hardheaded is what his dad had always said he was.

"I'll have this fire going again in a minute, and you'll warm up." Though in his opinion, the furnace was doing a more-than-adequate job of keeping the house comfortable. Then again, he was used to the weather. Kelly was from California, the land of sunshine and warm winters. "So what prompted you to go on a possum-hunting spree?"

She glared at him. A smart man would have given her room. Chance moved closer, enjoying the fire that spit from her green eyes.

"I heard a noise, okay? It sounded like someone was trying to get in the house. You took the dog with you, so I had no way of knowing if it was friend or foe."

"Out here we don't get much crime. I can't remember the last time someone had a break-in. Except for the time Jed Cooper got drunk and ended up crawling in bed with Mrs. Hartly."

He saw the smile tug at the corner of her mouth and had the strongest urge to press his lips there.

"I take it Mrs. Hartly didn't welcome him?"

"Nope. Neither did *Mr.* Hartly. Sheriff ended up tossing them both in the slammer—Mr. Hartly and Jed Cooper."

"So Cooper ended up sleeping with a Hartly, after all." Her eyes were losing their terrorized, petulant look.

"Yes, though come to find out, he didn't have designs on Miz Hartly. He was just too drunk to remember which house was his and went in the wrong door."

"It wasn't locked?"

"Not likely. Mine never are."

"Oh, God, I'm glad I didn't know that earlier. The only thing that kept me halfway sane was believing an intruder was going to have to bust a lock to get in." She stopped, frowned, then her gaze darted to his. "It *wasn't* locked. I remember now. I was so worked up I didn't notice."

He told himself to keep his hands in his pockets.

He found himself reaching out, rubbing his palms over the fleecy sleeves of her robe. "There's no danger here, Hollywood."

"Try telling that to my brain. I doubt that thirty years of caution, double dead bolts and sophisticated security systems will just disappear. The idea of a door being unlocked makes me feel really vulnerable."

"Then we'll lock them."

"I'd appreciate it." She sighed and dropped her forehead onto his chest. "I can't believe I fired that gun. I could have killed that poor possum."

"If you weren't intending to shoot, why take the gun in the first place?"

"If I had the business end of a shotgun pointed at me, I'd run like crazy. I figured any other reasonably sane person would do the same."

"You ought to know folks intending harm are not always that sane."

"I wasn't thinking much at all past the pounding of my heart. And I feel so stupid for overreacting."

He steered her to the couch. "Critters can make a lot of noise. And you're not used to the place yet."

"I live in Bel Air where there's hardly any space between the houses. Out here it's not as if you can just run over to the neighbor's house if you get scared."

"But they'll always come running if you call."

"A person could be hacked to pieces by that time."

He chuckled. "What an imagination."

"I'm a city woman. I'm not used to creatures charging me."

"Mmm." He put his arm along the back of the

couch, pleased when she didn't move away. "The varmints deserved to be scared, but the trash can was an innocent bystander."

Her head whipped around, her blond hair swishing across the shoulders of her robe. "You're going to dine on that for a month, aren't you."

He grinned. "At least for a day."

"What would it take to get you to keep this to yourself?"

His gaze dropped to her mouth.

"Chance," she warned.

He sighed and seriously considered the possibility that he might combust from the desire rushing through him. He didn't move back, though. "Shame on you. I'd never blackmail you into a kiss."

He brushed his lips over her temple. She went absolutely still, but she didn't pull away. Progress, he thought.

"But persuasion. Now *that* I would do." He lowered his head slowly, nibbled on her bottom lip, watched her green eyes darken. "How am I doing, Hollywood?"

She exhaled a shaky breath. "Oh, the hell with it." Her words were whispered against his lips as she cupped the back of his neck and pulled him to her, diving into a kiss that bypassed seduction and went right to carnal.

Chance's head spun, and it took a minute to get his wits. He'd meant to take it slowly, to cherish her. Yet the power of her kiss whipped through him, and before he even realized his intentions, he had his arm around her waist and tugged her beneath him on the sofa.

"Wait," she whispered, panting.

His heart pounded. Their bodies were aligned the way a man wants his body aligned with a woman's—breasts to chest, pelvis to pelvis.

He pulled back and his lower body pressed even more snugly against hers. He barely suppressed a groan. "Too fast, right?"

Her chest rose as she took a breath. Her green eyes studied him. "You know this is a bad idea, don't you?"

"It feels like a pretty good idea to me."

Her lips curved. "You're not going to have your way with me, Doc. But darned if I'm going to waste a prime opportunity like this. Once more is all you get. And watch your head."

He'd forgotten about his stitches. As the blood pooled painfully in his loins, he let her urge him back down. This time, though, he'd had enough forethought to master his control.

She wanted a kiss that was fast and physical. He could tell by the shallow breaths she took, the lift of her hips against him, the strength of her arms around him.

He gave her slow. Very slow. If she was only allowing him once more tonight, he was damned well going to savor her.

Kelly shifted, moaned, then gave herself up to the kiss. She didn't know what possessed her to encourage him this way. But she was in heaven. She'd never had a man kiss her like this, so deeply, so thoroughly. His lips and tongue danced with hers, softly, carefully, gradually asking for more.

She felt every inch of his body against hers, and despite her better intentions, she pulled him harder into the cradle of her thighs, torturing them both. It was pure madness, but she couldn't seem to find the moral strength to stop.

He came up for air, studied her for a long heart-stopping moment, then framed her face in his hands.

"That was for you," he murmured, his lips hovering bare inches above hers, his blue eyes dark and intense, his gaze steady. "And this one's for me."

Wild, was all she could think as his lips closed over hers once again. And powerful. This was a kiss a woman wouldn't soon forget. Raw and sexual and still somehow tender. It felt out of control, yet she knew he was completely aware, that he wouldn't take either one of them someplace they weren't yet ready to go.

With skill and expertise he kissed her until colors exploded behind her closed lids, until she barely knew her own name. And then he was easing away.

She nearly embarrassed herself and begged for more. She managed to subdue any more outbursts. Thank goodness he had enough willpower for both of them. If it had been up to her to stop, she didn't think she could have done it. She'd have dived in and suffered the consequences tomorrow.

"That was…something." Understatement. She'd had no idea a kiss like that existed. Steve had been her first and only sexual experience, and he'd *never* done anything that came close to that…the unrestrained frenzy, that barely controlled feast of the senses that was somehow as tender as it was savage.

Lord help her if she had let Chance go farther. She might not have survived.

"Yeah, it was." He eased off her and sat up, pulling her with him. "And I'm not going to apologize for it."

She used the momentum and stood, putting some distance between herself and temptation. "I don't recall asking you for an apology. I had as big a part in this as you did."

His lips curved slightly. "And you did your part very well."

She was trembling, but she still smiled. She couldn't help it. He was too cute. And too sexy. And too tempting. "Well, I'm not doing it again, so don't get any ideas."

He studied her for a long moment. His gaze was lazy, but she didn't fool herself. He was a man who noticed the smallest nuance of emotion, cataloged it.

"What do you do for fun, Hollywood?"

She frowned, not trusting this switch in the conversation. "What do you mean?"

"You know. Fun. Playing—aside from killing the trash cans. Do you golf? Quilt? Run naked through the park?"

She blinked, sure he was kidding about that last part. "I used to play the piano."

"Used to?"

"Yes, used to. I work a lot, okay? What is this about, anyway?"

"It's about that kiss." He came up off the couch like a sleek panther who had his prey in sight.

Kelly stepped back, realizing *she* was the prey, and

nearly fell over the coffee table. His hands were right there to steady her, though, to draw her in.

"I'm willing to bet that was the first real kiss you've ever participated in. And that's a crying shame."

"Oh, for Pete's sake. I was married."

"Doesn't matter. I'm thinking your education is lacking."

"Are you saying—"

He put a finger over her lips. "No, I'm not saying you didn't do it right. Baby, if you did it any righter, we'd both be burned to a crisp."

"Then what?"

"You deserve to do it more."

"With you, I suppose?"

"I'm available." He gave her a smile filled with sensuality. "You've missed out on a lot because of that smart brain, haven't you."

She opened her mouth to deny, then closed it. He was right, and they both knew it. Her intelligence had set her apart from others for most of her life. It hadn't been until recently that she'd felt as though the rest of the world had caught up to her, that she hadn't felt so different.

He brushed a fingertip against her jaw. "It's going to be my pleasure teaching you to play. And for the record, we *will* repeat that kiss."

Her jaw went slack, and for the life of her, she couldn't find any words.

"Night, Hollywood." He stepped around her, leaving her confused and yearning and belatedly piqued, with nothing more for company than a dark Christmas tree and a merrily crackling fire.

What in the world was wrong with her? Standing there like a dope while he *told* her what they were going to do, decided what *she* needed. All in a tone that was practically a sensual threat.

And when in the world had that type of behavior become acceptable, causing intense giddy excitement deep in her belly? She clutched the lapels of her robe, annoyed.

Oh, who was she kidding? She *wanted* him to be her tutor.

And damn it, she was going to get a grip and stop these nonsense thoughts right now. No good could come of them.

She didn't have time to play. She was a grown woman with responsibilities.

Responsibilities that she was failing, she reminded herself, and that was breaking her heart.

Chapter Six

Kelly overslept the next morning, something she couldn't remember ever doing before. The strain of hunting possums and raccoons must have done her in.

She dressed as fast as she could, hating to be bare naked for even the few seconds it took to take off her gown and pull on jeans, wool socks and two sweaters. Didn't anybody around here believe in using their heaters? She was going to find that damned thermostat and set it at a decent temperature.

After a quick trip to the bathroom to freshen up, she made her way to the kitchen, following the sound of Jessica's high-pitched voice mingling with Chance's deeper one.

Maria was bustling around the kitchen, wielding a spatula, which she used to both punctuate her words and scoop breakfast from the skillet on the built-in stove.

"Mommy!" Jessica shrieked. "Maria made snowman pancakes. Come see. You could have some, too. Kimmy wanted ears, but snowmen don't have ears."

Kelly moved forward, her gaze snagged by Chance's slow sensual smile. The image of them practically wrestling on the couch flashed through her mind, and she was annoyed when she felt the heat of a blush stain her cheeks.

Well, darn it, she didn't know how to act on the "sort of" morning after. She had no yardstick of experience with which to measure.

Hoping to cover her reaction, she met his knowing smile head on, then dragged her gaze to her children, responding to Jessica's volley of words.

"It's okay if snowmen have ears," she said to Jessica, though she didn't imagine Kimmy had voiced such a request. But, oh, how she wished she had.

"Which is exactly what I thought," Maria said, presenting a plate to Kimmy that held a pancake in the shape of a snowman with ears.

A smile peeked out of Kimmy's closed lips. She folded her pudgy fist around the fork and dug in.

With a pleased expression on her face, Jessica watched her little sister like a mother who could barely contain her pride.

Kelly's throat seized. To cover the reaction, she dropped a kiss on the head of each of her daughters and smiled her thanks to Maria, who merely waved the spatula as if to say it was no big deal.

"Sit, Dr. Kelly." With amazing efficiency, Maria had a steaming mug of coffee in front of Kelly before she could even ask. "I'll have you a plate in a jiffy."

"I'm fine with just coffee."

"Won't do you any good to argue," Chance commented. He, too, had been watching the unique byplay between the little girls. "Maria believes in feeding folks whether they want it or not. Might as well give in gracefully.''

Maria set a plate of pancakes and sausage in front of Kelly and pointed the spatula. "Eat. Breakfast is the most important meal. Doctors should know this and not have to have an old woman remind them.''

It smelled wonderful, and eating it gave Kelly something to do rather than worry about her daughters or squirm in her chair and flash back on carnal kisses and sensual threats.

"Mommy, did you hear that scary noise last night?''

Kelly's gaze darted to Chance, then back to Jessica. "Um, what did it sound like, honey?''

"Like a big, big firecracker. You 'member when Joey DeLuca's brother did the bad firecrackers at the street party and the policemen came and taked him to jail? That's 'zactly what it sounded like.'' She punctuated this with a definitive bob of her head.

"I'm sorry it woke you. Were you scared?''

"Yes.'' She forked pancakes into her mouth, licked syrup from her lips. "But I forgot and fell asleep again.''

"That's good.''

"So did you hear it, too?''

"Mmm-hmm. A raccoon was rooting around in the trash, that's all.''

Jessica frowned and thought about that. "Does a raccoon sound like a firecracker?''

"Uh…no. That was probably me. With the shotgun.''

Jessica took a breath as though inhaling the whole

world, her expression utterly scandalized. "Did you *kill* the poor thing?"

As drama queens went, Jessica was right up there with the best of them. And now Kimmy had stopped eating and was waiting for the answer, too, accusation creeping into her eyes.

"Of course I didn't kill it. I didn't even mean for the gun to go off." She tried desperately to think of a way to put a more mature nonchalant spin on the tale. "Which is a very good reason why we should never, ever play with guns." There. Give a lecture and throw them off the scent of the conversation.

Chance's slow grin didn't bode well for successfully dropping the subject.

"Actually, girls, it was a possum *and* a raccoon. Your mother was very brave to investigate marauding critters in the night. Fortunately she missed by a mile. Murdered my perfectly good trash can, though," he added with a smile that rivaled the Devil's.

"Thank you so much for your input, Chance."

His grin grew even wider. "You're quite welcome, Kelly."

Jessica giggled and Kimberly smiled. Maria covered her mouth, no doubt hiding a smile, and glanced at the telephone as though she couldn't wait to start punching in friends' numbers.

Great, Kelly thought. Between the girls and Maria, the story would reach town before she'd even clocked in for work.

THE CLINIC WAS BUSIER than usual, and Kelly was actually falling behind. She was used to doing exams and medical histories—as the doctor—relying on the clerical staff to keep the paperwork straight. Now *she* was the clerical staff.

For the first time in the month she'd been here, the pile of charts and ringing phones were flustering her.

And damn it, every blessed soul who walked through those doors had heard about her run-in with the raccoon, possum and trash barrel.

As she ushered Mrs. Beecham into the examining room, the old woman patted her hand. "I imagine your wits are pretty shaken after last night, dear."

Kelly forced a smile. "I'm fine, Mrs. Beecham." *For the fortieth time today.* "It was really a very small incident. Let's get this shoe off so the doctor can take a look at your foot, shall we?"

"Yes, it's been hurtin' real bad." She patted Kelly's arm this time, not ready to give up the subject, even for pain. "It's no wonder you got scared. A person can't expect you to take to country life right off. You'll get used to it, dear. You might want to have some lessons with the shotgun, though. Some of 'em give a mighty kick, but you'll catch on quick enough."

"Thank you, Mrs. Beecham. I'll be sure and do that." She went through the standard procedures of checking vital signs and writing them on the chart for Chance, feeling thoroughly demoralized that a little old lady could obviously tote a shotgun and hit her target blindfolded—while Kelly was a danger to anyone in the area. Including the trash cans.

Despite her irritation with being at the juicy center of the grapevine, she noted that Mrs. Beecham's blood pressure was higher than usual, and in listening to the heart sounds, she detected a slight murmur.

She jotted a note on the chart, stopping before she automatically added a recommendation for meds and a consult with a cardiologist. That wasn't her job.

"The doctor will be right with you."

"Thank you, dear. I hate to be a bother."

"No bother, Mrs. Beecham," Kelly said gently. It was a wonder the woman could still walk. Her toe was inflamed and raging with infection.

She glared at Chance when she met him in the hall. He wore tight blue jeans, boots and a white doctor's coat with his name stitched over the breast pocket. It made her mood even darker that he looked so sexy.

He held up his hands in a gesture of innocence. "Don't look at me. I didn't tell a soul. Honest." He was entirely too smug and doing a bad job of hiding it. "Go holler at Maria. She's the one who burned up the phone lines this morning."

"I'm not going to holler at your housekeeper." She slapped a chart against his chest, which he scrambled to catch.

"Mrs. Beecham's in room three with an ingrown toenail. It's inflamed and pretty well embedded." She glanced at her watch. "You've got half an hour before your next patient. That should give you time to extract the nail. And double check the heart sounds, would you? I detected a slight murmur. I don't think it's anything to worry about, but you might want to refer her to a specialist."

He saluted and grinned. "Yes, ma'am. Sure I can't talk you into taking on some of these patients?"

"I told you, I'm not licensed to practice in Montana."

"Easy enough to fix."

She shook her head. "I'm only interested in part-time work. When the girls and I are ready, I've got a full caseload waiting for me in California."

She saw his brows draw together and felt a warning tug in the pit of her stomach. That kiss last night had shifted their relationship. When you locked lips with a man and ground pelvis to pelvis, things were bound to change. But she hoped he wasn't pinning any long-term expectations on the sexual desire that flared between them.

Granted, it was powerful. But it was hormones, just hormones. Nothing could come of it. Their lives simply weren't geographically compatible.

Pretending not to notice the stillness that had come over him, she said, "Mrs. Beecham's waiting. And, Chance? Try not to enjoy my city-girl discomfort too much, would you?"

His expression relaxed into a devastatingly sexy smile. "I'll defend you to the teeth to the very next person who mentions it."

Let him have his fun, she thought. There was bound to be a way to turn the tables on him. And once she found it, she'd jump on it gleefully.

CHANCE HAD NEVER seen anything like it. Word had finally spread that there was a new doctor in town—a woman doctor. He'd lay the blame at Maria's feet—or rather her phone announcements, which were more effective than a newspaper headline.

Since morning, a steady stream of cowboys had trickled in with minor complaints.

And every one of them had offered to give Kelly private shooting lessons. She was being a good sport about the constant reminders of her escapade, but he could tell she was starting to simmer. And damn it, if anyone was going to give her target lessons, it was going to be him.

He still wasn't sure he understood why she'd misled them all this past month, why she couldn't have just fudged a bit, told them she was a doctor who was burned out and didn't want to practice for a while. No big deal.

Then he remembered where she came from, what she was running from—prying people who fed on her misery. She'd had no privacy. Keeping a low profile was the only way she knew to ensure that people were held at a distance. She didn't trust easily. He wanted to fix that.

He leaned a shoulder against the door of examination room two and folded his arms across his chest, watching the graceful way she moved and the simple smile she flashed. It could make a man go from zip to hard in an instant.

No doubt Rusty Tate was thinking the same thing. Hell, a dab of antiseptic ointment and a bandage could fix the little scrape on the cowboy's wrist, he thought, as he watched the man hold out his arm for Kelly's inspection and eat her up with his eyes.

These knee-jerk flares of jealousy were new to him. He'd been watching her all morning, charming every one of the patients who came in—most of them male, several of them twice her age. She was efficient and friendly, gentle and kind, compassionate and capable.

An odd pressure built up behind his sternum, emotions he couldn't define. There was an anxiety inside him, something that lurked just beneath the surface and made him want to sweep her off her feet and hold her to him until he could figure it out.

He kept coming back to one specific feeling. That Kelly and her girls were like a moment out of time that might never come again. And if he wasn't careful, they'd slip through his fingers.

He'd thought he was perfectly happy as a bachelor. His life was full with family and friends. And ever since the geezers had started their matchmaking shenanigans, he'd had to dodge all manner of women.

Then Kelly had come to town with vulnerability in her eyes and sass in her mouth. And he'd started to think that bachelorhood wasn't all it was cracked up to be.

Damn it, he was falling for Kelly Anderson and her girls like a ton of bricks. He could actually see himself spending his life with them.

Kelly was stubborn and brave and so obviously out of her element here he found himself wanting to hover over her.

Kelly was having none of it, though. Oh, sure, they'd shared a couple of hot kisses and the chemistry between them was undeniable, but that didn't mean she was simply going to fall into his arms and live happily ever after with him.

Her heart had been wounded.

He wanted to be the man to heal it.

Pushing away from the door, he strolled into the examining room.

"A man could get his feelings hurt when folks he's tended to half their lives come in wanting to switch physicians."

"Hey, Doc," Rusty said, the tips of his ears turning red.

"Tangled with some barbed wire, did you?" He stood next to Kelly and examined the wound, which was swollen and festering. A little peroxide and it would have healed on its own.

"Yeah. It's just a scratch, you know, but Wyatt sent me down here to get a tetanus shot. Kept going on about lockjaw, which didn't scare me," he said, glancing at Kelly. "But he told me I was off the payroll till I got it done."

"Wyatt's a smart employer."

"Yeah, well, I figured I'd just come on over and have Doc Anderson jab me in the arm and be done with it so Wyatt'd get off his high horse."

"Mm-hmm. But we don't jab. And this type of shot is best given in the hip."

Chance bit back a smile at the panic in Rusty's eyes. The cowboy glanced at Kelly, who was holding a syringe, then back at him.

"Uh...begging your pardon, Kelly...uh, Dr. Anderson. But if I've gotta drop my drawers, well, maybe..."

"Relax, Rusty," Kelly said. "Despite what you've heard, I'm only the doctor's assistant."

"But I heard you were a doctor."

"In California. Here, I'm an assistant. So I'll just

step out and give you some privacy." She handed the syringe to Chance. Obviously she was astute enough to have read the expression on his face when he'd first come into the room, because amusement was dancing in her green eyes.

"Don't jab," she said only loud enough for him to hear.

"Wouldn't dream of it," he countered, and watched like a man under a spell as she walked out of the room. When he turned around, he noticed that Rusty appeared equally entranced.

"Some woman," the cowboy said.

"That she is. Roll up your sleeve."

"I thought you said it had to be in the butt."

"Changed my mind."

Rusty shook his head and pushed up the sleeve of his undershirt. "Can I ask you something, Doc?"

"Sure."

"You got designs on her?"

"Maybe. This'll burn." The needle went in so easily Rusty didn't flinch. Chance congratulated himself on his restraint.

"You best define that 'maybe' or you're gonna be butting heads with a whole lot of competition."

Chance withdrew the needle and swabbed the injection site with alcohol. "Fine. Do me a favor and pass the word to my competition that Kelly Anderson's off-limits."

"Uh-oh," Rusty murmured.

"Uh-oh what?"

Rusty nodded toward the door. Chance turned and saw Kelly standing there.

And she was not a happy woman. She gave him a look that nearly seared him where he stood.

"I'm off the clock, Dr. Hammond." She put an extra emphasis on the *Dr. Hammond* part, reverting to a formality that they were miles beyond. He knew he'd have to do some serious backtracking here. "I'll speak with you later."

"Man," Rusty said when she'd left the office. "You're in the doghouse now."

WHEN HE GOT HOME that evening, he had the urge to tiptoe into the house, then chastised himself. It was his house, damn it.

He heard music and followed the sound to the living room. A fire burned in the fireplace and the lights on the Christmas tree were lit. The scent of pine and smoke mingled with the delicious smell of whatever Maria had in the oven. Kelly was at the upright piano playing a melody he didn't recognize. She was good. Better than good.

An overwhelming sense of right washed over him, a feeling he hadn't experienced since he was a boy. For the first time since he'd bought it, this house felt like a home.

And it had a lot to do with the woman making beautiful music on his grandmother's piano.

He took off his hat, wondered if he should toss it into the room and see if it came sailing back at him.

She glanced up and noticed him standing there, her fingers faltering over the keyboard only for a second. Aside from that slight hiccup, she continued to play…and held his gaze at the same time.

"I'm annoyed with you," she said at last.

"Yeah, I figured as much."

She turned her attention back to the ivories, playing as though it was second nature to her. "I'd forgotten how music soothes me."

"And is it working in my favor?"

A smile flirted with her lips. "I don't know yet. Do you play?"

Fairly certain he wasn't under siege, he moved into the room and sat beside her on the piano bench.

"Chopsticks. I could probably mangle 'Jingle Bells.' The piano was my grandmother's. I keep it for sentimental reasons." He watched her slender hands, hands that could sew incredibly fine stitches in a head wound and make beautiful music, too. "Where are the girls?"

"Upstairs with Maria. I was banished from the room. Maria gives 'funner' baths."

"We'll get you up to speed in the fun department."

She merely raised a brow. The melody she played so smoothly was working its way under his skin, a hauntingly sensual tune he couldn't place. He only knew it evoked emotions.

"I don't recognize this song."

This time, she did smile. "I went through a song-writing phase when I was twelve. This is one of the results. I'm surprised I remember it."

Amazing. He wondered what it had been like to compose music at twelve and enter medical school when she was still in her teens. The knowledge in her head must be incredibly vast, far superior to the average person's, yet she never let on, never talked above anyone.

"You are one of the most intriguing women I've ever known."

She glanced at him but didn't comment. Was this mysterious air deliberate? Or simply the self-assurance of a very strong woman? He imagined it was the latter.

"Tell me about your family," he said.

"You ask a lot of questions." Her dark-blond hair fell forward as she concentrated on the notes of a new tune she'd segued into.

"I'm trying to distract you from being mad at me." He brushed back the lock of hair that was hiding her expression and was pleased to see her smiling. "It's working, isn't it."

"You're an impossible man. Despite the fact that I'm not interested in a relationship—with *anyone,*" she said, her fingers coming down harder on the keys, "it was wrong of you to warn them off."

"I apologize."

Her hands stilled on the keyboard. The abrupt absence of sound pulsed louder in his ears than the wail of a siren.

She turned slightly and looked into his eyes, obviously gauging his sincerity and searching for his usual flirting.

He gazed right back at her steadily. Because he was genuinely sorry. "I had no right to talk about you when you were out of the room."

She nodded, and he could see in her eyes that she wasn't a woman who held a grudge.

"Thank you. I accept your apology. Just don't let it happen again."

"Scout's honor."

"I didn't ask the dog to make a promise, and you already told me you were never a Boy Scout. Pick another."

"Okay. On *my* honor."

"That one I do trust."

She said it so easily he was momentarily startled into silence. It was a compliment he hadn't expected and one that made his ego soar. He wanted to just sit here and bask in her praise, but he was afraid something would break the tenuous truce, the easiness between them. He didn't often catch her with her guard down.

"Play something else." He winked at her. "You said it soothes you. I'd hate to break the spell."

"Why? Are you going to make me mad again?"

"God, I hope not."

Kelly put her hands back on the keys, sifted through the files in the music niche of her mind and began to play a Christmas carol. She didn't consciously think of the notes. They simply flowed.

"You're really good."

"Thank you. Once I learn something, I rarely forget it."

"You must have run your folks ragged."

"Mmm. That's probably why I was an only child. I guess I was a handful." It felt good to play the piano again. It had been years since she'd taken time for it.

"You're close to your parents?"

"Very. Dad gave up a medical practice and became

the CEO of his own computer firm. He's still a work-aholic and swears he'll never retire. You'll meet him because he'll be out here for Christmas. I told you my mom's gone. I miss her.'' She still caught herself wanting to pick up the phone to share something exciting with her mother, only to remember she couldn't.

It was the same with Candy. Even though Candy was very much alive, she was no longer the best friend Kelly had believed she could count on. There were moments when she forgot, was halfway to the phone before she remembered. And remembering hurt all over again. She'd had so few chances to build friendships. The one she'd managed had turned out to be false.

She felt Chance's hand sweep over her back, a gentle touch that soothed, and her thoughts shifted back to her childhood.

''Sometimes I think my parents didn't know quite what to do with me. My curiosity was insatiable. I wanted to learn and absorb as much as possible, as fast as possible. It was like an obsession, you know?''

''Mmm, not really. I was a hell-raiser and would just as soon have skipped school. Luckily, learning came easy for me and my grades were mostly *A*s. But it wasn't an obsession.''

She glanced at him. He did have the look of a bad boy about him. He had, in fact, an innate gentleness he probably wasn't even aware of.

He had his elbow propped on the piano, his head resting on his palm, his gaze steady on hers. She couldn't recall ever being the absolute sole center of a man's attention before. It made her nervous.

She stopped playing, took her hands off the keys and put them in her lap. The cut on his head was healing nicely, she noted. She'd need to remove the stitches in a couple of days. "I bet you were the kind of kid who brought home every wounded animal and nursed it back to health."

"Yeah." He smiled. "It was tough on my image."

Kelly chuckled. "I didn't run into many stray animals in the city." The fire warming her back and the smell of the tamales Maria was making for supper lulled her into a realm of serenity she wasn't used to feeling.

"I was plagued with this constant sense of anxiety, like a scream was right there at the back of my throat, and if I didn't keep going, faster and faster, if I stopped to take a breath, the scream would rip loose. We had quite a family argument when I wanted to skip high school and go right into college."

He straightened and his thigh pressed more firmly against hers. "Did you ever outrun the scream?"

"Yes. Age and accomplishments tamed the restlessness."

He lifted one of her hands from her lap, brushed his thumb over her knuckles, then brought it to his lips and pressed an incredibly soft kiss there, his gaze holding hers.

She drew in a breath, held it. A different kind of scream was building now. A sexual one. "What was that for?"

He shook his head. "You never really were a kid, were you."

"Of course I was."

"Were you? Do you have little-girl memories of tea parties with your teddie bears or playing jacks or jumping rope?"

No, she didn't. She raised a brow. "You know about these things?"

"Heck, yes, I have two sisters. I've attended my share of tea parties."

She'd told herself she could resist his charm, had every intention of doing so. But when he looked at her with those blue eyes filled with an intoxicating mixture of mischief and sensuality, she felt as though she was drowning.

Without thought, without will, she leaned toward him, mesmerized, drawn by a power she simply couldn't fight.

"Mommy! Mommy! We had bubbles in the bathtub!"

She jerked back to her senses. Jessica and Kimmy charged into the room, their hair caught up in pigtails, their robes flapping behind them like Zorro's and Batman's capes.

Chance turned and caught Kimmy up in his arms as Jessica scrambled onto Kelly's lap. Scout skidded on the rug and nearly slid under the tree.

"Bubbles?" Kelly looked up at Maria. The woman stood beaming in the doorway, the front of her shirt and the knees of her pants wet.

"Yeah. And Scout sneezed in the water and got it all over the place and on Maria, too."

"I can see." She sent an apologetic look toward the housekeeper, who was fast becoming a surrogate grandmother to the girls. "I'm sorry about that."

"Oh, a little water is nothing. The tamales will be ready to come out of the oven in ten more minutes. Everything else is in the refrigerator. I will see you both in the morning."

"Bye, Maria!" Jessica shouted, obviously filled with more energy than she knew what to do with. She bounced on Kelly's lap and pressed a couple of keys on the piano. "Play 'Jingle Bells,' Mommy."

Kelly looked at Chance. Kimmy's pigtails were caught high on her head like puppy ears, brushing the underside of his chin. "Didn't you say that was one of your specialties?"

He grinned at her. "I said I *mangle* it. You play and we'll sing. Kimmy can hum, though I doubt we'll be able to hear her over Jess's voice." He shot a look at the dog. "Scout, you keep quiet. He can't carry a tune," he said in a stage whisper to the girls.

Jessica giggled. Kimmy peeked around him at the dog as though assuring herself there were no hurt feelings, then glanced up at Chance with a smile so sweet Kelly held her breath, certain words were about to follow.

Chance, too, seemed frozen in suspense.

Then Kimmy laid her cheek against his chest and the moment was lost.

Kelly wanted to weep.

And when Chance cupped a hand gently over her baby daughter's cheek and dropped an absent kiss to the top of her little head, Kelly knew she was a goner.

"Play, woman," he said. "We've got five minutes before we have to rescue the tamales."

Kelly plucked out the opening notes of "Jingle Bells," and tried like mad to rein in her emotions.

Nothing got to a woman faster than a man who openly adored her kids.

Chapter Seven

Since Chance didn't keep regular office hours, Kelly's work schedule was pretty much part-time and she was home the next day by early afternoon. Maria usually stayed for the rest of the day and prepared dinner, but she'd left early today.

Kelly went into the kitchen and opened the refrigerator, wondering if she should fix dinner for the four of them or just for herself and the girls. After all, she was a boarder in Chance's house, not living with him. It wasn't up to her to make sure he ate.

Oh, she didn't know what to do, and she disliked uncertainty. It left her wide open for the restlessness to set in, the anxiety that pushed her to stay busy every moment.

She'd been doing better lately, taking more time for herself and the kids. But the screams sneaked up on her sometimes. She'd told Chance she'd outrun them. But she hadn't. Not completely.

The back door opened and Chance came in, bringing the cold air and the fresh scent of winter with him.

Kelly slammed the refrigerator door like a thief caught raiding the pantry.

"Hi. Uh, I was just thinking about dinner. Maria left early. I really should go to the market, bring in more groceries. We never set any guidelines or rules about the division of supplies and—"

"Kelly?"

"What?"

"It's Thursday."

She frowned, wondered if she'd missed something. "So?"

"So, Thursday nights are dinner at Brewer's."

"They are?"

"It's tradition."

"Oh. Of course. Well, you go on ahead and I'll just fix supper for me and the kids."

He laughed. "Oh, no, you don't. I took plenty of flack on Thanksgiving when you bowed out. I'm not sitting through Thursday dinner with half the town glaring at me."

"But we're not a couple. Why would they expect us to come together?"

He took his hat off, tossed it on the counter and walked toward her. Kelly had an urge to back up. He looked like a man with something on his mind. And that something might well be her.

When her back hit the counter, she was forced to stop, trapped with nowhere else to go. "Chance—"

"It's a little late to worry about folks thinking we're a couple. They'll think what they want regardless of the facts. But you're *not* sending me off to face that pack of meddlers alone."

He sounded so horrified, she laughed, even though

she suspected he was putting on an act. "Really, Chance—"

"Don't make me have to resort to blackmail."

"And just what do you have to blackmail me with?"

"Two little girls. Want me to call them now so we can take a vote?"

"You're a heartless man."

"Ah, no, Hollywood. I've got plenty of heart." His gaze was like a caress. Then he winked. "It's courage I'm lacking. You can't send me off to face everybody on my own. They've unofficially put me in charge of seeing to it that you and the girls join all the festivities."

She sighed. "What should I wear?"

He stared at her as though she'd asked him whether the snow was going to melt in the next five minutes. Well, darn it, she didn't know what people in Montana wore to Thursday-night dinner.

"You're fine just as you are." His gaze traveled over her with a masculine appreciation that was impossible to miss. "Nice tight jeans, flirty little sweater."

She tugged at the hem of her sweater. It was cropped, designed to only reach the waistband of her jeans. At the moment she felt as though it was a bikini top—and totally inappropriate for a Montana winter.

Chance grinned. "It's no wonder you're always cold. You're not wearing enough clothes. Not that I've got anything against a lack of clothes, mind you."

"Chance?"

"Hmm?" His eyes were still checking out the front

of her sweater and jeans, obviously waiting for her to shift and expose part of her middle.

"You better quit while you're ahead."

"Mmm. Progress. I like being ahead. I'll go get the girls. You put on some boots. There'll probably be dancing."

"Wait," she said to his retreating back. "You never said anything about dancing."

"Girls!" he hollered, ignoring her. "Grab your coats. We're going to town for dinner. Burgers and milk shakes."

Her jaw dropped and she put her hands on her hips. "Now you've done it. Do you cheat at cards, too?" She refused to be swayed by that sexy dimple in his cheek.

"You said I was ahead."

"You just lost all your points."

He laughed. "I like you, Kelly Anderson."

"Yeah, well the jury's still out on you."

BREWER'S SALOON was lively and festive, filled with townsfolk and decorations. Garlands hung in loops from the bar with shiny red balls hooked onto them, the pictures on the walls were wrapped in bright paper to look like presents, and a ten-foot tree stood in the corner with gifts already beneath it.

As they walked past the door to hang up their jackets, an irreverent moose belted out "Grandma Got Run Over by a Reindeer" and went right on singing, its furry mouth flapping. Chance figured they'd be pretty sick of the song before the night was over, since the crazy thing was motion-activated and there was a lot of motion in here.

He took Jessica and Kimberly's coats, but kept his eye on Kelly. He could tell she was nervous and he wanted to put his arm around her and assure her everything would be fine. He suspected that would offend her sense of independence, though, and send her into her ruffled-feathers mode.

He had an idea being a child prodigy had set her apart from people—she'd have been too old for kids her age and too young for the peers on her intellectual level. Tough life.

He helped her off with her coat, noted that she'd added a T-shirt under the flirty sweater.

"Aw, you put another shirt on."

"I didn't want my belly button to get frostbite."

"I'd have kept it warm for you."

She gave him a look of warning, which he had no intention of heeding. He figured it was best not to tell her that just yet.

"Shall we go into the back room and be sociable?"

She shrugged. "You lead, we'll follow."

He slung an arm around her shoulders. "My sisters told me never, ever to take off across a room and leave a lady to follow behind."

"Yes, well, I appreciate their forward thinking and all, but we don't want to give the wrong impression and encourage Ozzie and his friends. Are you sure they're actually trying to matchmake?"

He laughed. "Let me give you a few examples." With his arm still casually around her shoulders and his head close to hers, he pointed.

"See Wyatt and Hannah Malone over there? Hannah was Wyatt's mail-order bride, except he didn't advertise for her. The geezers did." He nodded to the left. "Ethan and Dora Callahan? The old guys arranged for Dora to show up at a bachelor auction. Ethan was on the auction block. She bought a date for his daughter—who he didn't know he had."

He shifted her slightly as he continued his examples. "Eden and Stony Stratton? They conspired with Stony's housekeeper to skip town and brought Eden to replace her. Eden had come to have Stony get her pregnant."

"Did he know?"

"Nope. But everybody else in town did. Then came Emily and Cheyenne. You were here when they got together."

"How was that matchmaking? Emily came to town so Cheyenne could help her once she delivered the twins."

"Yeah, but she was expecting to rent the place next door to him. Ozzie, our esteemed mayor, leased her a house that had burned down two years ago and accidentally on purpose listed Cheyenne's address on the papers."

"Very devious."

"Mmm. And seeing as how Ozzie and your father are old pals…well, you might as well just go with it."

"I told you, my father wouldn't have been party to something like that."

"Maybe that's so. Doesn't mean it'll stop the meddlers from scheming."

Nikki Stratton came running up with Ian Malone in

tow and took both of Jessica's hands in hers as though they were ladies greeting each other at a garden-club tea social. Then the little girl included Kimmy in the welcome.

What a darling child, Kelly thought. Sensitive and kind.

"Did Marcy come?" Nikki asked Jessica, her tone both reverent and excited.

Kelly and Chance glanced at each other. *The angel.*

"She always comes," Jess said.

"Oh, good. Come on. We get to pick out some songs on the jukebox." All four kids took off like rabbits racing toward a lettuce patch. Jessica skidded to a halt, glanced back at Kelly.

"Is it okay, Mommy?" she asked belatedly.

"Go on," Kelly said. She wished she could be as relaxed and social as her children.

What in the world was the matter with her? She'd rubbed elbows with movie stars, attended medical seminars with some of the country's top physicians, gone to benefits that cost a thousand dollars a plate. Yet she was nervous as a cat over the prospect of walking into a friendly diner with jukebox music and a sign over the bar admonishing folks to watch their language as this was a family establishment.

Why the nerves? she wondered, and immediately knew the answer. These people were genuine. No air kisses here. They gave warm hugs and meant it. These were people who cared, who could easily matter.

What if she didn't measure up? If she failed? What if they decided she was a bad mother because she couldn't provide whatever it was Kimmy needed in order to heal?

"You doing okay, Hollywood?"

She glanced up at Chance, snagged by the concern in his eyes and in his voice. She could have evaded the question. She didn't.

"I guess I'm reliving some old insecurities. As a kid I told myself that it didn't bother me when everyone stared at me when I came into a room. I was always different. Too young or too brainy. But it did bother me. I was always out of step, isolated."

He gazed down at her, pushed a lock of hair behind her ear, raising chills on her arms that made her shiver in response. "You're not alone here, Kelly. And if anyone stares it's only because you're so beautiful they can't help themselves."

"Oh, I am not."

He went very still. "You really believe that, don't you?"

"I'm passably pretty, that's it."

From the corner of her eye, she saw Ozzie Peyton heading their way.

"You gonna monopolize the girl the whole night, Chance, or let the rest of us enjoy her?"

Chance grinned and put his arm around her again. "You go get your own date, Ozzie, and leave mine be."

Kelly slipped out from beneath Chance's arm. My gosh, hadn't they just been discussing this matchmaking business? Why in the world was he encouraging it?

"It appears my boss is suffering delusions—must

be that wound on his head—because he seems to forget I'm *not* his date.'' She glanced at Chance. ''Remind me to order up some tests for you, perhaps a CAT scan. That short-term memory loss is starting to worry me.''

When she set off across the room, Chance took a breath, puffed out his chest and grinned. ''Don't you just love a woman with sass?''

''You bet,'' Ozzie said, all but rubbing his hands together gleefully. Things were going right well, even if he did say so himself. He glanced at Chance, said slyly, ''Glad to see you admitting it.''

''Admitting what?'' He was still watching Kelly, who was cooing over Emily and Cheyenne's twins.

''What you just said, boy. That you're in love with a woman with sass.''

That brought Chance's attention back. ''I didn't say that. It was a rhetorical statement.''

''Hmm. Must be these old ears gettin' bad, you bet. Guess I'll just get on over to the cigar-smokin' section before Iris closes it on us. It's roped off so the young'uns don't stray in, but that don't seem to please the woman. Lloyd's gonna have to have a talk with his missus, you bet. You coming?''

''Those cigars are bad for you.''

''Now, Doc, we don't inhale.''

Chance grinned at the man he'd known since he was in diapers. ''I'll pass, thanks. Better keep myself healthy since I'll likely have to be doctoring you.''

''Humph. I'm strong as an ox and more ornery than a mule. Won't catch me in the doctor's office. And you ought to be worrying about your own self. You forgotten all your courtin' skills?''

"If I thought you were maligning my masculinity, I might have to ask you to step outside."

Ozzie laughed and slapped him on the back. "Nothing wrong with your manliness. A little slow if you ask me, you bet."

"I don't believe anybody did ask you."

Ozzie's vivid blue eyes twinkled. "Ever known that to stop me?"

"No, and to tell the truth, it confounds the hell out of me."

Ozzie laughed again and took himself off to join his buddies in the cigar-smoking section, and Chance walked toward Cheyenne Bodine, who was standing with several of their neighbors.

As usual at these sort of get-togethers, the men gravitated to their own corner—closest to the billiard tables and smoking section—while the women congregated in the other. He noted that the ladies had pulled Kelly right into their fold.

"Evening, Chance." Wyatt Malone, holding his one-year-old daughter, Meredith, glanced at Chance's temple where the wound was starting to heal. "You figured out yet which end of the donkey to stay away from?"

"Very funny."

"Emily feels bad," Cheyenne said. "She's the one who advertised and turned the production into such a big thing."

"Tell her to rest easy. Besides, it was the preacher

who actually started everything. And Ethan who brought the ill-behaved donkey to begin with.''

Ethan Callahan grinned and wagged his fingers at his daughter, Katie, as she toddled by. ''Any fool knows not to stand behind a donkey.''

''I imagine the boy was distracted,'' Ozzie said from several feet away. He passed out cigars to his three buddies, Lloyd, Vern and Henry. ''What do you think, boys?''

Chance noticed that all his friends were looking at him with a sort of amused compassion, expressions that seemed to say, ''Give it up. We happily lost the battle. Now it's your turn.''

Chance was fairly certain he'd like to give up the battle, but he didn't like being in the hot seat this way. He'd do things in his own time.

''Did we come here to eat or what? Hey, Madean,'' he hollered to the waitress. ''You taking orders yet?''

''As soon as you sit your butt down, sugar, I'll be glad to.''

Over the course of the night, as he visited with his friends and ate burgers and fries with Kimmy in his lap and Jessica racing around with the neighbor kids, he gave Kelly plenty of room.

He could tell she was still a little annoyed with him for telling Ozzie she was his date, but he was confident she'd get over it. Too bad there wasn't a piano handy.

As the music started and couples began to pair off on the dance floor, he watched Kelly from across the room.

Amused, he noted the mix of expressions that crossed her face when Iris and Vera obviously asked her something of a personal nature. He'd seen this reaction before. She was alternately shocked and suspicious, then understanding would dawn and she'd relax her guard.

Just as she did now.

She'd be fine, he thought. People in California were different from folks in a small Montana town. And for all her impressive accomplishments, Kelly's world had been narrow.

Chance had plans to expand it.

Having held himself back for as long as he could stand it, he crossed the room, catching her alone for the first time that evening.

He stopped in front of her, put his hat on and tugged the brim low, then held out a hand. "Dance, Hollywood?"

He saw the automatic refusal, an endearing distress, the vacillating between want and nerves. He took the decision out of her hands, pulling her up and right into his arms.

A country two-step number was playing on the jukebox, and he slid into the rhythm, his thighs brushing hers until she was forced to step back or trip them up.

"I don't know how to do this dance," she said in a fierce whisper.

He pulled her more tightly against him. "Just follow me."

"Chance—"

"Shhh." He rested his cheek against her temple, torturing himself by holding her so that their bodies were stuck together tighter than adhesive on a gauze bandage. "Just ease into me, feel me."

"I'm feeling a little too much of you."

He chuckled against her hair. "Yeah, but you're picking up the steps like a pro, aren't you." He felt her chest raise against his.

"There is that. You're going to start more rumors."

"I can handle it. How're you doing?"

"With the dance or with tonight?"

"Since I'm sharing the dance, I guess I mean tonight."

"Well, I think I'm getting the hang of this incessant penchant your neighbors have for giving and receiving personal information."

"Figured you would."

"It's kind of refreshing, you know? People are genuinely interested in me. Nobody's looking to exploit my children in a newspaper, to snap photos of the child who doesn't speak, to pounce on and pour over the story of tragedy while they drink their morning coffee."

"Ah, babe. I can't begin to imagine how difficult that must have been for you."

Her hand crept up behind his neck, gave a squeeze as though thanking him for his understanding.

The thing was, he didn't really understand. He knew very little about that part of her life. She kept it clutched to her like a fist around an heirloom handkerchief.

"I'm surprised you don't hold it against our local grapevine for passing along tales about the shotgun and possum thing."

"That's different. Everyone who mentioned it also offered to give me shooting lessons. I haven't encountered a single person in this community who doesn't give three times more than he or she takes."

He led her into a turn, pleased that she followed effortlessly, hardly aware that she was partnering with him as though they'd been doing this for years, instead of minutes. She felt slight in his arms, his hand practically spanning her back, but he knew she was strong.

The juxtaposition, delicate and strong, excited him.

All the kids were out on the dance floor now, bouncing and bobbing and laughing as only the young could do. Needing a minute to calm his libido, he released Kelly and scooped Kimberly into his arms to dance her around the floor.

Kelly looked momentarily surprised, unsure of what to do now that she was unpartnered on the dance floor. But Nikki and Jessica took care of that in an instant, grabbing her hands and twirling around like exuberant ballerinas, drawing her right into their realm of fun.

"How's it going, sweet cheeks?" Chance asked Kimberly, and rescued his hat before it fell off. She had her little arms around his neck like a baby boa constrictor.

"You having fun? How about a dip?" He bent forward in an elaborate dip, holding the back of her head. Her round blue eyes lit like twinkling stars, and tiny teeth showed beneath her shy smile.

He brought them back upright and gave her a smacking kiss on the cheek. "I know, you're thinking I'm an excellent dancer, but you'd just as soon hang with the younger set. I can take a hint. Here we go, we'll do a smooth switch, and your mama won't know how we managed it.''

He swung Kimberly down, steadied her on her little feet, then swept Kelly right into another fast two-step, leaving behind a trail of laughter as the kids giggled and hopped in a crazy sort of jumping-bean dance.

''Honestly, Chance. You don't give a woman time to catch her breath.''

''Hey, if I give you time, you think too much.'' He pulled her close to him and she didn't object. Holding her like this called for a slower step, more romance.

He changed the tempo, brought their linked hands between them, holding hers close to his chest. The brush of her breast against his forearm nearly drove him mad.

It was the most incredible madness he'd ever experienced.

''This is much better.''

She glanced up at him. Her gaze went to the brim of his hat, which nearly touched her forehead, then settled back on his eyes, his mouth.

He groaned and pressed his cheek against hers. He wasn't made of steel, and if she kept looking at him like that, he was really going to give the folks of Shotgun Ridge something to feed their grapevine.

''Chance?''

''Shh, I'm concentrating.''

She giggled. It was such a foreign sound coming from her, such a surprise, he eased back to look at her.

''What?'' he asked.

She shook her head, then said, ''Thank you for bringing me tonight. I've had...fun.''

He smiled, slipped his hand beneath her hair and urged her head to his shoulder again. "That's a good start, Hollywood. A very good start."

KELLY WOKE UP with a start. Her heart thumped and for a moment she was disoriented. As her eyes adjusted to the dark, she realized someone was in the room.

Kimmy stood next to the bed. Just stood there like a tiny wooden doll. Silently. Staring.

"Oh, honey, what is it? Did you have a bad dream?" She held out her arms. "Want to come in here with me?"

Kimmy climbed into bed and snuggled.

"Brr," Kelly said, tucking the quilt around both of them. "Cold, huh?" She stroked Kimmy's forehead and soft hair, soothing.

Please, God, tell me how to break through this silence.

"I wish you could tell me your dream," she whispered. Her heart pounded as words ran around and around in her head. Could she choose the right ones? Should she even try? What if she made matters worse? Brought up a horror that Kimmy might not even be thinking about?

Snow drifted outside the window. The clock on the maple nightstand ticked so loudly in the silence, the sound seemed to echo off the walls.

"Remember how I taught you to share your toys?" Kimmy nodded and Kelly gently stroked her silky hair. "You've always been so good about it. It's good to share your hurts, too, you know. Sometimes, if you let somebody else have a little bit of the hurt, it won't be so bad. Maybe it'll even go away. You can tell Mommy anything,'' she whispered.

Kimmy's only response was to snuggle closer to Kelly's side.

Kelly wanted to weep. Instead, she pressed a gentle kiss to her daughter's baby-soft cheek and whispered, ''It's okay, sweetie. You sleep, now. Mommy's right here.''

She wrapped her arms tightly around her daughter, feeling frustration, and a love so fierce and deep it was a wonder it didn't seep right out of her body and into her daughter's.

Tonight Chance had insisted she needed to have fun. And she'd nearly agreed with him. What could she have been thinking? It was Kimmy who should be having fun, frolicking like a four-year-old, shrieking and screaming and giggling.

Kimmy was what Kelly needed to concentrate on.

KIMBERLY SQUEEZED her eyes closed and wished with all her might that the bad thing would go away. But the bad thing kept coming back, snapping at her with big teeth and looking at her with mean eyes. *Swish. Swish. Pop.*

Kimmy felt a scared whimper way down deep in her tummy, but it wouldn't come out. She 'membered the bad thing, though. Daddy looked like he was playing. And then he fell down. She should have called for Mommy. Mommy could have fixed him 'cause she was a doctor. She'd told Auntie Candy that.

''Dear, God, Candy! Why didn't you hit the circuit

breaker? Knock him loose? Call for me? I could have done something! Three minutes sooner and I could have saved him!"

Auntie Candy cried and Mommy and her didn't talk anymore. Mommy was mad at Candy. Kimmy thought Mommy was prob'ly mad at her, too, but Mommy didn't want to say.

She shouldn't have waited for Auntie Candy to stop laughing. *"Quit joking around, Steve. You're such a cutup."*

Kimmy had felt scared but didn't know why. She should've talked when Daddy fell down.

Now she couldn't. If she opened her mouth, nothing came out. She guessed that was prob'ly okay. If she didn't talk, she couldn't be guilty ever again. The bad thing couldn't happen. Nobody could die.

Chapter Eight

Chance watched the efficient way Kelly moved around the clinic, keeping busy, as though afraid to slow down lest some sort of beast catch up to her.

She was clearly avoiding him, and that ticked him off. He'd been sure they'd made more progress last night at Brewer's. Hell, she'd even admitted she was having fun.

One step forward and three steps back.

Grabbing two cumbersome medical chests—the drug chest and the metal box containing the heart monitor and diagnostic equipment—he strode toward Kelly and stopped at the front desk.

"Grab a coat, Hollywood. Today's the day we do house calls."

"Today's the day *you* do house calls."

"Come on, Kel, I need you. I've been out to the Thurmans a couple of times now. I'm fairly certain Ella's got mitral valve prolapse, but she refuses to come in for an echocardiogram. She's not symptomatic—no irregular heartbeat, no migraines, chest pain or panic attacks." Although Mrs. T did claim the urge to bash Mr. T with the skillet now and again. That probably didn't count as panic attacks.

"So, since she won't come in, I'm thinking she should at least err on the side of caution and take a dose of antibiotics if she plans to have any dental work done. I'd feel a lot better if I had a second opinion, though."

"Chance—"

"Come on, Kel. You might have fun." The minute he said it, her eyes clouded. Damn it, he was going to find out what was the matter with her. And having her cooped up in the truck with him as he made rounds to folks who couldn't or wouldn't come in for treatment was an opportunity he didn't want to pass up.

"Please?" He'd resort to begging if he had to. "Come with me and see what country doctoring's all about." As a professional, he was pretty certain she wouldn't be able to resist. He'd seen her immediate interest when he'd described Mrs. Thurman's symptoms.

"I need to get home to the girls," she hedged.

"We'll be back by noon. You're on the clock until one, anyway."

She lifted a brow. "Are you pulling the 'I'm the boss' routine?"

He grinned. "I can. I was hoping you'd be curious enough that I wouldn't have to. You're a doctor." He held up his hand when she automatically opened her mouth to argue. "Being a doctor's not just a job. It's a mission. It's part of who we are. Are you going to stand there and deny that I'm right?"

Kelly heaved a sigh and picked up her coat. "You know, it's an ugly trait to gloat."

"I'll work on it." He held the door open for her, locked it behind them, then stowed the two chests in the back seat of his pickup and helped her into the cab.

She noted that he also had survival gear behind the seat and wondered if he'd ever had to use it. The possibility of getting caught in a blizzard wasn't such a stretch of the imagination. Montana was a completely different world than California.

Snow had fallen last night, but not enough to make the roads impassable. When he started the engine, music blared from the radio, and he quickly reached to turn down the volume.

Kelly glanced over at him with a small smile. "You know that'll ruin your hearing."

"Naw. I figure I'll outgrow playing it loud before it does any damage."

The knobby tires of the truck crunched over a muddy pile of snow as he pulled out onto the street. Sunshine glinted off the decorations on the town Christmas tree, its branches fluttering gently in the breeze. Patches of snow clung to the roofs of the church and the redbrick courthouse.

Kelly loved looking at the wintry scene. The snow was beautiful, nature's way of upholstering the countryside in a blanket of white. Puffy clouds hung low in a sky so blue it nearly hurt to look at it. She just wished something so pretty wasn't so doggone cold.

She hadn't had an opportunity to drive around much since she'd come here. Partly because the less she drove on ice-slick roads, the better she liked it, and because she simply hadn't given any thought to exploring.

"So where are we going?"

"About twenty miles up the road and over a ways. Barney Heppermill's wife called this morning and said Barney was having chest pains. He insisted it wasn't bad enough to call an ambulance, so we'll check on him first."

"I didn't take a call from a Heppermill," she said, glancing at the chart on the seat between them.

"That's because she called in on the radio before you got in." He glanced over at her. "Now, you want to tell me what happened to you between last night and this morning?"

"I don't know what you're talking about."

"Yes, you do."

She sighed. Chance was the type of man who got information out a person if he wanted it. He wouldn't let up until she told him.

"Kimmy had a bad dream. At least I *think* that's what it was. I feel so damned impotent when it comes to my little girl."

"Do you think it has to do with the accident?"

"I suspect so. But I don't know. I don't want to probe or bring up bad memories if that's not what she's thinking about. On the other hand, I don't want to ignore it if that *is* what's plaguing her little mind."

He drove easily, with his wrist resting on the steering wheel, his free hand ready in case he needed to do some fancy maneuvering—or wanted to reach across the cab of the truck and offer comfort.

Kelly's younger daughter had wrapped herself around his heart, and he didn't think she was going to turn it loose anytime soon. He wanted to help her. Maybe it was none of his business, but he wanted to make it his.

"Do you know how much she saw?" He knew what electrocution could do to a person. It wasn't a pretty sight.

"No. I wish to God every day that I did. I don't know what kind of monsters I'm fighting."

"Will you tell me about it?"

She turned her head, gazed out at the snow-covered prairie. She was silent for so long he thought she wouldn't answer. At last she spoke.

"Steve was in Candy's garage, playing handyman, of all things. The man wouldn't even change a light-bulb, yet he decided to play Mr. Fix-It, God only knows why."

"Candy. Your friend, right?"

"My ex-friend. Steve's girlfriend."

"I don't get it. Why the hell would he take his daughter to his girlfriend's house?"

"Oh, we were *all* there. It was very civilized, you see. Candy wasn't just my best friend, she was Jessica and Kimberly's godmother."

"Ah, hell."

"Steve wasn't there for a tryst, though—they kept that secret well hidden. I didn't find out about the affair until the funeral. In any case, we were there for dinner and I was in the kitchen putting together a salad. Steve went out in the garage to check out the earthquake strap Candy needed for the water heater—

a code requirement when someone's selling their house, which she was. I have no idea what possessed him to pick up that old drill motor and try to install the part himself. Maybe he wanted to impress Candy with other skills besides the ones in the bedroom. Who knows?''

She tugged the lapels of her coat closer, and Chance reached over and turned up the heater.

''I heard Candy screaming. I ran out, and Jessica followed. Kimmy was standing by the workbench, half-hidden, terrified. When I saw the burns on Steve, I knew right away what had happened. I started CPR, but he was already gone.''

''So Jessica saw, too?''

''A little bit. My body was pretty much covering him while I was trying to get his heart started again. I remember that Jessica was hiding her face in Candy's skirt, but Kimmy was just staring. She was in the garage with them the whole time. She could have been playing somewhere, maybe not seen it all. I asked Candy and she didn't know, couldn't remember. She was watching Steve. When the electricity got hold of him, she didn't realize that's what was happening. She thought he was goofing around.''

He didn't know what to say to her. He'd seen death, but it hadn't been as personal as this. He wondered if he would be as strong as Kelly if he'd gone through such a horrific nightmare.

And he wondered if he had what it would take to heal her, show her that life wasn't about betrayal, that there were people you could trust, count on. That she didn't have to carry the whole load alone.

She held so much on her slender shoulders it was a wonder she didn't bow from the pressure. But she was stubborn, led with her chin. As he imagined she'd done all her life—as a gifted kid who'd been isolated because of her special qualities, instead of embraced, and as an adult who'd seen her dreams shatter.

Kelly knotted her hands in her lap, trying not to dwell on what she couldn't change, wondering if she would ever stumble on the answers she needed. She felt Chance's hand cover hers. So warm.

The squeeze of compassion nearly released the emotions she tried so hard to repress. She wanted to turn her hand over, link her fingers with his. But she kept her hands locked together, and after a minute, Chance removed his.

"Not much farther," he said. They turned off the highway and traveled several miles on a road that was hardly more than a rut in the snow.

A run-down house came into view, the porch sagging, the yard littered with rusted-out cars missing engines and all manner of parts.

"Barney's in the salvage business," Chance said.

They climbed out of the truck, retrieved their equipment and mounted the porch steps. Chance gave a perfunctory knock on the storm door with its ripped screen, then walked in as though he was visiting family and sure of his welcome.

Kelly followed, glancing around. She noted the soiled slipcover that didn't quite hide the sag in the middle of the couch. The Christmas tree that held a place of honor in front of the picture window, a single flat package beneath it wrapped in aluminum foil and tied with a red ribbon. For all its sad state, the house was neat and clean, and quaintly festive.

"How're you doing, Barney?" Chance asked.

"'Bout the same. Been better. Got me a fierce pain right in here." The old man pounded a fist on his sternum. "Not sure if it's the old ticker or not."

"Well, let's have a listen." Chance took the stethoscope Kelly handed him. "Barney, this is my assistant, Dr. Kelly Anderson."

"Mighty pretty for a doctor. Puts you to shame, boy."

"That she does." He listened carefully to the heart and lung sounds. Systolic and diastolic pressure were fine, and sinus rhythm was normal. Plenty of gastric activity going on, though.

"Mm-hmm," Chance said, "just as I thought. You been eating Bessie's chili-pepper stew again?"

"She makes the best in these parts, you know."

"I know. But you gotta go easy on it." He turned to Kelly. "I think a GI cocktail will do the trick."

"Do you have the meds for it?"

He winked. "A good Boy Scout always comes prepared."

"You weren't a Boy Scout."

"Damn. How come I keep forgetting that?"

She shook her head and hid a smile.

He turned back to his patient. "Barney, have you developed any allergies to medicines since I saw you last?"

"Not a one."

"Well, then, we're going to give you a semi-pleasant-tasting mixture of stuff with fancy names that's basically a supercharged antacid. It'll stop the heartburn, and stomach pain. Should have you feeling up to snuff in no time at all."

After Barney took the medicine, Kelly helped pack up their equipment. She saw the older man press a five-dollar bill into Chance's hand.

"I'll send more when business picks up a bit."

Chance shook his head. "Not necessary. Your account's paid up." The man started to object. Chance put his hand on Barney's shoulder, saving the man's pride. "That medicine came to me as free samples from the drug reps. I'm not out any money. We really are square." He shook Barney's hand. "You all have a Merry Christmas."

As they walked back to the truck, Kelly was silent, thoughtful. She'd known Chance's well of compassion was huge. Seeing him in action was eye-opening—and humbling.

His type of doctoring was vastly different from anything she'd encountered in California, where insurance companies dictated the level of care and a seven-minute office visit cost a hundred bucks.

She thought about the five-dollar bill Chance had tucked into his pocket without even looking at it. She'd already known he treated first and worried about insurance second. It was a wonder his practice could keep its head above water, but amazingly enough, it did just fine.

"That was sweet, what you did for Barney."

He shrugged. "Bessie was driving an hour one way to work in a garment factory. They recently made some cuts, and her job was one of the first to go. She's been trying to save up to buy her granddaughter a tricycle.''

Kelly felt her heart squeeze and had the most over-whelming urge to send the Heppermills enough money to buy that tricycle and a Christmas ham, too. Some-times she got so caught up in her own problems she forgot to count her blessings.

''What made you decide to practice here in Shotgun Ridge, rather than the city?''

''I didn't like the politics in the city. And the vio-lence got to me.''

''Where did you go to school?''

''Harvard.'' He saw her eyes widen and nearly laughed. It amused him that he had a snootier educa-tion than she did, and she was the one who worked in a big city.

''Money's never been an issue in my family. My dad made a good living ranching, and my mom made a fortune selling her art. When I went off to college, they moved into the city so Mom could open a gal-lery.''

''And you said you had sisters?''

''Two of them. Both older, married with kids, living in the city.'' And continually poking at him because of his single status.

''Dad retired from ranching—which was taking its toll on his body. They sold the ranch because I didn't need it. I'd already settled on my choice of career, and the ranch was too big, required time and effort that I wouldn't be able to give it. All I needed was a small piece of land to keep a couple of horses, someplace close to town and my medical practice.''

"So did you always know you'd come back here to hang out your shingle?"

"Probably in the back of my mind. I interned in a busy trauma center where gunshot wounds were the norm." If he closed his eyes, he could still hear the inconsolable screams of mothers who'd lost sons and daughters.

"It got to where the patients I *didn't* save outnumbered the ones I did. And that's not what I'd gone through a decade of schooling for."

Checking his mirror, he pulled into the next lane to overtake a slow-moving pickup, giving a wave to the driver as he passed.

"Everything was so impersonal," he continued. "I kept flashing back to Dr. Monroe coming out to our house when my sister fell under the tractor and nearly lost her leg. Doc was there before the ambulance. He worked like a demon to save the leg. He talked Lisa through the pain, held her hand, distracted her by asking about school and the calf she was raising to enter in the county fair, and about the boy in town who was sweet on her. He'd known all those things about my sister. I couldn't say the same for a single one of the patients who came in and out of my emergency room."

He saw an elk poised at the edge of the road and took his foot off the gas in case the animal decided to dart across the highway.

"Anyway, the ambulance took Lisa to the hospital where a surgeon repaired her leg, but I remember the gratitude we'd all felt toward Dr. Monroe for being first on the scene. And when she got home, he was the guy who came out to the house to check on her, to drink coffee and talk about life. That's what I wanted. To know my patients and care. Not have them just be a chart with symptoms. So when Dr. Monroe retired, I took over his practice.''

Kelly watched Chance easily maneuver the truck around a pile of slushy snow in the road. His looks didn't fit the image he'd just described, but the man did. The man he was inside.

He was content. She tried to remember if she'd ever been content. She remembered the nagging discontent she'd felt in her house of stone with security gates and high walls fencing them in from outsiders. She'd been half joking when she'd asked her dad where the old days had gone, the ideal depicted on old TV westerns about families and communities and a simpler life.

It was alive and well in Shotgun Ridge.

And Chance Hammond, the long, lean, flirtatious cowboy doctor was the modern-day epitome of her deepest, most exciting fantasy.

She shook herself out of those thoughts, wondered where in the world they'd come from. She hadn't spent ten years and over a hundred thousand dollars to become a surgeon just to walk away from it.

Then again, nobody was asking her to.

THEY SAW SEVERAL more patients over the course of the morning, and the innate doctor in her had Kelly digging in and participating, not merely assisting. She'd agreed with Chance's assessment of Mrs. Thurman's heart murmur and was touched when the woman insisted she take home two jars of homemade blackberry jam.

These house calls had nothing to do with money and everything to do with people's lives. Sometimes the patients simply wanted to talk. And Chance knew what to talk to them about.

Just like the man who'd been his role model.

As they headed back to town, Kelly felt a satisfaction she rarely felt—even after a successful surgery. Because in surgery, most of her patients were simply bone, tissue and organs. She didn't know if their grandmother had recently died or if their pipes had frozen last winter or if they were still waiting for somebody to show up and fix the roof. She didn't know their anniversary dates, their kids' birthdays or that crazy cousin Al had set tongues wagging last Halloween when he'd taken his flasher costume a little too far.

She thought about young Sally Thurman, a girl of about fourteen, who'd watched Chance with shy adoring eyes the whole time they'd been there.

"Do you have problems with female patients falling for you?"

"More often, it's the females who *don't* want me taking care of them. You remember Emily Bodine's reaction over a prenatal examination." Though he'd ended up delivering her babies, after all.

"She went to school with you. That's understandable."

He glanced over at her. "I wouldn't mind if a certain assistant fell for me."

"Your ego astonishes me."

"Hey, I'm a man who knows where he's been and where he's going...and what he wants."

She didn't need him to interpret that for her. The intensity in his blue eyes said plenty. She couldn't deny the chemistry between them. That hot kiss on the couch had stirred her up and she hadn't settled since. It was clear he wanted her. She just wasn't sure what to do about it.

"Why don't you roll down the window and let that cold air cool you off?"

He laughed. "So what did you think, Hollywood?"

"About?"

"About country doctoring."

This was much safer ground. It was tough being this close to him in the cab of the truck.

"I honestly didn't think this sort of thing existed. You're a good doctor, Chance." The compliment was sincere and she waited until he'd acknowledged it. "You made me consider my own patients. I don't think I can ever go back to being the doctor I was."

"What do you mean?"

"I'm not talking about skill. I'm talking about the verbal communications, the caring, the families. I'm always in such a rush. I check on one patient, then walk out and directly into the next examining room, the other one forgotten for the moment. A different face, a different ailment. They're scared when they come to me. I don't always take the time they need. But I can tell you one thing I've learned from you. When I go back, I won't be letting my patients leave my office until all their questions have been answered."

"Don't sell yourself short. You've got good people skills, Kelly. I saw you in action."

"Today, yes. That was a wonderful eye-opening experience, and I think it's going to make me a better doctor. You know, I was terrified to come to Montana." She hated to admit that aloud, but this seemed to be a day for honesty and unburdening.

"Alone, with just the girls. Not knowing anybody. It was so drastic, perhaps an act of desperation, but I took a chance. It could have gone either way with the kids."

"It seems to be having a favorable impact on them."

"Yes. I'm selling my house in Bel Air." The admission came out of the blue. What was it about this man that got her talking and not knowing when to shut up. She gave a mental shrug.

"I was afraid to make any significant changes after Steve died, didn't want to put any more on the girls than they could handle. That's why coming here was such a big risk. But now that we've been away, distanced ourselves from the familiar environment, I think selling will be easier. I called a real-estate agent and told her to list the house."

He looked at her, his expression guarded. "Are you staying here, then?"

"No, I didn't mean..." Damn. The sizzle between them was definitely going to cause problems. It was giving them all an unfair sense of hope. "I was going to buy another one closer to my office in Los Angeles," she admitted quietly.

"I see." His tone was just as quiet.

Silence filled the cab of the truck for the rest of the trip back to the clinic. Kelly wanted to probe, to ask him what he was thinking, but that would leave the door open for reciprocal questions.

She didn't have any answers of her own to give back if he asked the hard ones.

Chapter Nine

From the warmth of the kitchen, Kelly watched Chance in the corral where he was brushing a beautiful reddish-brown horse. Jessica and Kimmy followed on his heels like puppies every time he took a step.

Since it was Saturday, the clinic was closed and Chance had announced it was the day for chores— which the girls promptly volunteered to help with.

He wore a pager and the CB radio was on, both in the barn and in the house. If he was needed, he was within reach.

That was the kind of man he was. Within reach. Someone to count on.

He was an innately masculine man, yet he knew the names of his patients' pets, had artwork of fairies on his walls and photos of babies on his tabletops.

The contrast between the man and his environment was endearing. And exciting.

And it was little wonder that the grapevine was alive and well, she thought. Everybody had a CB radio in their home and routinely listened in on neighbors' conversations.

Pulled by the scene beyond the kitchen window,

Kelly downed some pain medication, hoping to take the edge off the ache behind her eyes, then put on her coat and went outside to brave the cold.

The girls frolicking so close to that horse's hooves was making her a bit nervous. They were small, within easy kicking distance. She clearly remembered what had happened to Chance when he'd gotten behind the hooves of an animal.

She went to the corral fence, propped a boot on the bottom rung.

"Girls, don't get in Chance's way." *Don't get in the horse's way.*

"We're not in the way," Jessica said. "Chance is gonna let us have a ride on Lolly. Peppermint was too cold and wanted to stay in her nice warm barn for longer. Chance told us that. Can I feed Lolly some hay now, Chance? Please, please, please?"

Chance grinned and looked down at Jessica. She was dancing around as if she had ants in her pants. "Okay, but just a little bit. We don't want her to get too full. She gets lazy when she's full and then doesn't want to take little girls for a ride."

"Okay. Just a snack." She held out her hand with a few strands of hay in her palm, then turned her head, peeking out the corner of her eye, giggling.

"Don't be scared. She's a lady and ladies know better than to bite. It's not polite."

Jessica giggled again, then squealed. "It tickles!"

When Jessica squealed, Kimmy wrapped her arms around Chance's thigh and pressed her cheek against it. He reached down and stroked her hair. He'd noticed that Kimmy didn't always distinguish between a good scream and a bad one.

And it melted his heart that she'd grabbed on to *him*. The trust she was beginning to place in him was a true gift.

He lifted her up in his arms. "You want to ride?"

She shook her head.

"I do! I do!" Jessica yelled. Lolly's head jerked and Jess ducked.

"Whoa," Chance soothed. "There's a girl. Best not to hop," he said to Jessica. "Lolly'll think you're a rabbit. And she doesn't like to admit it," he said in a stage whisper, "but she's scared of rabbits."

That got Kimmy's attention. She took her face out of his neck and looked at the horse through different eyes, evidently speculating that the horse might not be so bad if she was scared.

"Aw," Jessica cooed. "I'm sorry Lolly. Don't be a'scared. We have a be-eau-tiful angel to watch over us and she can watch you, too, so the rabbits won't get you. Okay?" She gently patted the horse's leg with a mitten-covered hand.

"Well, now, since we have angels watching, I guess it'd be a good time to take a ride. What do you say, Kimmy? You look like a girl who's apt to change her mind. You want to ride on Lolly with your sister?"

Kimmy thought a minute, then nodded her head.

"Good girl. I'll be right here for you. Up we go." He put her on the horse's bare back, steadied her with a hand on her leg, then reached down and swung Jessica up behind her sister.

Belatedly he glanced at Kelly. "I guess I should have asked. Is this okay with you?"

"It's safe?"

"You can trust me." He was saying so much more. And he could see that she knew it. "I'll have my hand on them the whole time."

He walked beside the sorrel, one hand holding the lead rope, the other resting on both little girls' legs, ready to right them if they slipped. Lolly stepped daintily and slowly. Jessica beamed. Kimmy didn't beam, but her tiny smile was enough to touch his heart.

They made a loop around the corral, and when they came level with Kelly at the fence, he stopped, taking a good look. She looked a little pale, not her usual self. "You okay, Hollywood?"

"Other than freezing, I'm fine."

There was strain in her eyes. He raised a brow. "No fibbing to the doc, Doc."

"It's just a little headache."

"Did you take something?"

"Yes, Doctor."

He shrugged. "So sue me. I worry about people."

Her eyes softened and pulled him right in. He felt as though he could drown in those green pools.

"Why don't you go on in the house, curl up by the fire and let the meds kick in. I'll take good care of the kids."

He saw the immediate refusal spring to her eyes. He also saw that she desperately wanted to accept.

He reached out and cupped her cheek. "Go on, Kel. We'll be fine."

"All right. But I'll be just inside if anybody needs me."

What would she do if he told her *he* needed her? He watched her walk away, saw how straight she held her shoulders, how she took great care not to move her head.

"Again, Chance?" Jessica asked, bringing his attention back.

"Okay, once more around the fence, then we have to go do the dirty work and muck out some stalls."

"Yuck. There's a lot of poop in there."

"Yep. But Lolly gets pretty upset when her house is stinky."

Jessica giggled and leaned past Kimmy to pat Lolly on the neck. "Okay. We'll make it sweet for her."

"Atta girl."

KELLY COULDN'T REST. She kept looking out the window, watching Chance charm her children, bend down to speak to them, to laugh, to ruffle their hair. They followed him with adoring eyes.

Steve had never spent time like this with his daughters. He'd breeze in and say, "Hiya, kid." And that was about it.

He didn't read them bedtime stories or tease them into smiles or walk them around corrals on a horse.

The only reason Kimmy had been in the garage with him that fateful night six months ago was that Candy had overruled him, said yes when Steve said no.

God, how she wished for once she hadn't resented Steve's no's. She'd almost gloated when Candy had taken Kimmy out with them.

If only she could go back and relive that night. She'd have snatched up her babies and run as far and fast with them as she could, shielded them from grown-up tragedy.

Realizing she wasn't going to get any rest for fear of missing something wonderful and endearing, Kelly took a book and a lawn chair out to the yard and parked it several feet away from the corral so she could watch the interaction between the girls and Chance.

She shouldn't let it touch her so. That was dangerous. But she couldn't seem to help herself.

Besides, maybe the cold would freeze this headache out of her.

She started to object when Jessica took off toward the barn, chasing after Scout, but she made herself sit quietly because Chance was watching, too, and didn't appear to mind. Besides, none of them had noticed her sitting there, and Kelly decided that was just as well. It gave her the opportunity to simply observe.

Chance and Kimmy stayed in the corral with Lolly—who was moseying around loose. Kelly tried to relax, told herself that Chance would never put her children in harm's way.

"So, Kimmy, what do you think of Lolly?" she heard him ask. Without waiting for Kimmy, he answered for her, carrying on a conversation as though Kimmy was keeping up her end of the deal.

"You think she's a beauty, hmm? So do I. Want to know a secret? Lolly used to live in a bad place. The people who had her didn't take good care of her. When she came here, her heart was broken and she was sad and quiet and scared, and her ears drooped. My friend Stony fixed her, though. You've met him, remember? Nikki's dad. Well, he's what we call a horse whisperer. He talks to horses without ever saying a word. You understand how to do that, don't you?''

He shook out a saddle blanket and hung it over the fence, then picked up the hose he'd retrieved from inside the barn and hooked it to the spigot. "Sometimes people can say a lot without a single word. Doesn't make them all that different, does it.''

Kimmy was following him, listening intently, watching his every move. "Here, you hold the hose and I'll turn on the water. The trough's getting a little low, and we don't want Peppermint and Lolly to strangle themselves trying to get a drink.''

He stopped and gave Kimmy a wary look. "You're not thinking about squirting me with that hose, are you? Because I'd turn into an icicle, then I'd have to doctor myself. Oh, I forgot, your mom could doctor me. Do you let her doctor you? I bet you do. She likes that, you know. Likes being needed. Makes her feel like a 'can do' girl.

"That's why we have to let her take care of us. I tell you, I wasn't real happy letting her sew up my head when that old donkey accidentally kicked me, but she did a very fine job. Barely notice the stitches. See?'' He leaned down and shifted his hat so she could inspect the wound.

"What do you think? Think it'll leave a scar?''

Kimmy shook her head.

"That's good to know. I'd hate to ruin my good

looks.'' He stopped, glanced down at Kimmy and waggled his eyebrows. ''You think I'm conceited? Naw. I've just got healthy self-esteem. That means I like who I am, and if somebody called me a name, it wouldn't bother me because I'd know better. You ever had anybody call you names or say mean things? My two sisters used to call me names all the time.''

Kimmy turned to look up at him and the hose went with her, nearly dousing Chance's boots, but he smoothly directed the stream back where it belonged.

''Does that surprise you? It's okay, really. Because even if they teased me or called me names, my sisters still loved me.''

He placed a hand on Kimmy's shoulder, glanced into the trough. ''That's probably enough water, don't you think? Hang on a sec, and I'll go turn it off.''

Kelly smiled at the nonsense talk he kept up. She could see by Kimmy's expression that she felt as though someone was actually interested in her and not treating her like a baby.

Kelly tried to read, or at least pretended to. She didn't want Chance and Kimmy to know that she was eavesdropping. They still hadn't noticed that she was sitting here.

When snowflakes landed on her book, she looked up. Everything within her went still.

Kimmy was standing in the corral, her red mitten-covered hands held out, head back and tongue out, trying to catch snowflakes in her mouth. It was such a normal *kid* thing to do.

Chance noticed, also. And he stopped what he was doing, mimicked Kimmy's stance and waited for snowflakes to land in his mouth, too. Kimmy looked at him. Some sort of silent communication seemed to be taking place between them.

And Kelly was terribly, *terribly* afraid she'd just lost her heart.

Still grappling with that startling realization, she frowned when a van turned into the long driveway that led to the house. The interruption caused Chance to look over, finally noticing her sitting off to the side.

He glanced at the van that had the name of a florist on the side, then squatted next to Kimmy and called for Jessica, whispering in both girls' ears. The girls came running over to Kelly's side.

A young man got out of the van with an armful of flowers.

Flowers in the dead of winter.

"I've got a delivery for a Kelly Anderson, Jessica Anderson and Kimberly Anderson."

"I'm Kelly." She took the clipboard he held out to her and signed her name.

"These are for you, then." He handed her a gold box tied with a red bow. Through the cellophane window on the top, she could see what was inside.

Roses.

Speechless, hands trembling, she looked up and across the yard to where Chance was leaning against the corral fence, watching them. His black hat was cocked low on his brow, his denim jacket hanging open, an elbow propped on the wooden rail. A smile creased his sinfully handsome face.

Hearing the delivery boy speak, she dragged her gaze away, saw the young man hand a spray of daisies to Kimberly and a bouquet of sunflowers to Jessica, who was squealing and dancing and hugging the flowers so hard yellow pollen was smeared on her face. Kimberly was holding hers as delicately as fragile china.

Where in the world had he found sunflowers and daisies in December?

"Enjoy," the boy said, and jogged back to the van.

Kelly untied the bow and carefully lifted the top off the box. The heady fragrance of roses wafted up. Twelve of them. Velvety red ones. The color of love.

When Kelly looked up again, Chance was standing beside her. A lump rose in her throat. She hadn't felt this weepy this often in her entire life.

There were no cards with the flowers, but she knew who they were from.

"Why?" she asked.

"Just for fun. Haven't you ever gotten flowers for no reason? Just because?"

"I've never received flowers, period." She lifted the blooms from the box and buried her nose in them.

He gaped at her. "You're kidding, right?"

She shook her head.

"Not even for your prom?"

"I didn't go to a prom. And I bought my own flowers for my wedding."

"Damn it, Kelly. Are you telling me no little boy ever even gave you a wildflower?"

He sounded so indignant she put a soothing hand on his arm, chuckled. "It's okay, Chance. Did you ever give a little girl a wildflower?"

"Yes. Tina Lindenberg. Third grade. I was in love."

"And did she love you back?"

"Yes, until Cheyenne turned her head. She dropped me like a hot brick. It was those brooding Indian looks. The girls couldn't resist him. Took me two whole days to forgive him."

She laughed, because she imagined all the little girls hadn't been able to resist Chance, either. He had a charm that drew a female in whether she wanted to be drawn in or not.

What would it have been like, she wondered, to have gone through school normally, having little boys present her with bouquets of wildflowers, to go to classes each day, enjoy the fun of recesses and spit wads and passing notes when the teacher wasn't looking?

Instead, she'd been obsessed with going faster, higher, sooner, forever trying to stay one step ahead of the scream.

With the blooms held carefully against her chest, she gazed up at Chance and said softly, very softly, "Thank you."

He gently stroked the backs of his fingers over her cheeks. "You're welcome."

Yes, she thought, terrified. She'd definitely lost her heart.

KELLY MADE IT through church the next day, but it was getting more difficult with each passing hour to ignore her headache. She needed a dark room. And a bed. And some major drugs.

None of which she could indulge in at the moment. They were expected at the Malones' for Sunday dinner, and she had the girls to think about.

She hated to shush Jessica, but her daughter's exuberant voice was pulsing behind her eyeballs and radiating outward with each syllable.

"Why don't you go on to the Malones' without us," she said to Chance when they got home.

He laid the backs of his fingers on her forehead, studied her. "This headache's been building since yesterday. Are you prone to migraines?"

"Unfortunately, yes."

"On a scale of one to ten, how bad is this one?"

"I'll be fine."

"One to ten, Kel."

"Eight...and a half, maybe." *A twelve.*

"Why didn't you say something sooner?" He gently turned her by the shoulders and headed her toward the hall. "Let's get you to bed."

"I don't have time—"

"Yes, you have plenty of time. I'm in charge."

"The girls—"

"Will be fine with me. Jess? Flip on the television for a bit, okay?"

"But aren't we going to Ian's? Hannah's makin' Sunday supper, and me and Kimmy and Nikki are s'posed to sleep over with Ian. Mommy said it was okay. Ian's got a goat! And new puppies!"

"Don't worry. The plans are only going to change a little. Give me a couple of minutes to take care of your mom. She's got a king-size headache."

"Oh, no," Jessica crooned, just now learning something was amiss. "Are you okay, Mommy?"

"She'll be fine," Chance answered for her. He waited until Jessica took Kimberly's hand and led her into the den, then turned to Kelly once more and ushered her down the hall.

"If I had the energy, I'd object to your high-handed bossiness."

"Mmm, I'll give you a rain check, how's that? Now, we need to get you out of these clothes."

"I've got a headache, Chance. I think I can still manage to undress on my own."

He grinned. "That was one of those royal *we*'s. If you want to strip here, that's fine by me. I figured you'd prefer the bathroom, though."

She managed a wan smile, then grabbed a pair of sweats and disappeared into the bathroom. He wondered if the sweats normally doubled as pajamas. Probably. She was always cold.

But she was a trouper about it and most of the time hid her discomfort. As she'd done with this migraine. She was a damned good actress. And for some reason, that saddened him. How much of her life had been spent pretending?

He roamed the room, noticing how she'd put her stamp on it. Two books lay on the nightstand, one women's fiction, the other a psychology study on children and trauma. The roses he'd given her were on the dresser in an opaque green vase, the reflection in the mirror making them look like two dozen, instead of one.

He picked up a bottle of perfume that rested on a

crocheted doily, sniffed, then noted the name on the label, filing it away for future reference. It was the only scent he'd ever known her to wear, one that had invaded his dreams for the past month.

She came out of the bathroom, and he set the perfume bottle back on the dresser. He knew she'd caught him snooping, but he wasn't going to apologize. He planned to know a lot more about her, very soon. And he'd use whatever means he needed.

She stopped by the side of the bed. "I feel weird, um...with you standing there and me going to bed in the middle of the day."

"Well, get over it." He pulled back the blankets and quilt, and waited until she sat on the side of the bed. Her eyeballs were actually shaking, a clear indication that she was beyond the moderate pain stage and holding on by sheer stubbornness and willpower.

How the hell had she hidden this from him? From everyone at church, for that matter?

"What do you usually take?"

"Midrin. Then Fiorinal or Anaprox. I'm allergic to codeine. When I can't get the pain to respond to the regular meds, I invariably end up getting a shot of Demerol—as long as my dad's available to keep the kids."

Not husband, he noted. Her father. Interesting.

"Well, I'm here to watch them. If they still want to go to the Malones, I'll see that they get there. Then I'll go over to the clinic and get the pain medication." He stroked her temple, brushed her hair back. "Will you be okay?"

"Of course. I'm always okay."

He doubted that. "Lie back and close your eyes, Hollywood. I'll try to hurry."

On his return to the girls, he stopped in the kitchen and called Wyatt's cell phone. The Malones had stayed longer after church, and as it turned out, they were just heading home.

"I'm coming up on your place now," Wyatt said. "Why don't I stop by and pick up the kids, save you the trip?"

"Thanks, buddy. I appreciate it. Though I need to see if they still want to go, since their mom won't be coming."

"No problem. Won't lose anything by stopping in to check."

Chance disconnected and went to the den where the kids had managed to find an old black-and-white slapstick comedy on television.

Jessica looked up. "Is Mommy okay?"

"She will be as soon as we get some medicine for her."

Jess nodded. "She likes to have the room dark. The light hurts her eyes. Sometimes Grandpa comes cuz Mommy sleeps a long time."

"That's the best thing for her." He heard a knock on the front door and knew that Wyatt and Hannah would let themselves in. Good thing Kelly wasn't in the room to see that he'd left the door unlocked.

"And since your grandpa isn't here, I need to stay and watch over her. Do you still want to go home with Ian?"

"Yes," Jessica said, popping up off the couch when she saw that Nikki had come in with Ian and his parents. She grabbed her sunflowers and scooted right around him. "See my flowers? Chance got them for me. And Kimmy got daisies and my mom got roses."

While the other kids hovered and exclaimed over the flowers, Chance bent down to Kimmy, stroked a palm over her chubby cheek and gave a playful tug to one of the pigtails that sprouted out of the side of her head like floppy puppy dog ears. Her eyes were solemn as she gazed back at him.

Man alive, this little girl tugged at his heart. He remembered how she'd gotten homesick the last time she'd slept over with Nikki. But she was more used to them now.

"What do you say, princess? Do you want to go?"

She nodded.

"It's okay if you want to stay with me."

She hesitated, glanced at the bouquet of daisies she'd wanted to take to church with her that morning, then shook her head.

"Okay." He slid his wallet out of his pocket and took out a card. "I'm going to write my telephone number right here. See? If you feel sad you can call." Though he didn't think she knew how to use the telephone. "Well, if you don't want to mess with the phone yourself, Hannah or Wyatt will call me. You just show 'em this card with the number on it and they'll know what to do, and I'll be right there to get you."

She slipped between his knees and wrapped her arms around his neck. For a tiny four-year-old, she had a lot of strength in that squeeze.

And with her arms around him and her face buried

in his neck, she climbed the rest of the way into his heart.

My God. He was headed on a course where there was a real possibility his heart was going to get broken three times over.

She kissed his cheek, then snatched up her flowers from the table and ran off to join the other kids.

Chance stood and cleared the emotion from his throat. "Guess I lost out to the goat and puppies."

"Stiff competition," Wyatt commented.

"Yeah." He shook hands with Wyatt and kissed Hannah. "If Jessica gets anxious, show her how to raise us on the radio. Sometimes the girls just need to hear their mother's voice."

"That's a wonderful idea," Hannah said. "Don't worry. I'm happy to keep them for as long as you need. I'm sure they'll be fine."

Yes, but would *he* be fine?

Chapter Ten

When Chance got back from the clinic with the pain medication, Kelly was rolled in a ball on top of the blankets. She hadn't even had enough energy to crawl beneath the sheets and had slumped right where he'd left her.

She flexed her fingers on her skull in a futile attempt at massage. If she'd been a horse, someone would surely have had enough compassion to shoot her and put her out of her misery. But she wasn't a horse, a fact she greatly lamented at the moment.

"Kel," Chance said softly to let her know he was there.

"I'm awake," she whispered, and rolled to her back. "The girls?" she asked.

"They're staying the night at the Malones. I'll call and check on them later. If they want to come home, I'll pick them up."

"Thank you." She saw him uncap a syringe and nearly whimpered because relief was within sight now.

"You know this is best given in the hip."

Yes, she did. And she hadn't considered that. It was ridiculous to be apprehensive—if that was what she was feeling. She was having trouble defining the turmoil inside her. Under any other circumstances, with any other doctor, she wouldn't think twice about letting him give her a shot in her rear end.

Damn it. She hated like mad for anyone to see her weak.

Pain overruled embarrassment, though. She rolled to her side and lowered the waistband of her sweatpants far enough for him to give the injection.

"It'll burn," he said.

"I know." She appreciated the warning, though. This wasn't one of those shots that was a quick pop and over before you'd ever realized you'd been pricked. This one went in slowly. The burn gave her something else to focus on besides the pain in her head.

"All done."

"Thanks." She expected him to leave the room and was surprised when she felt the mattress dip, felt his arms slip beneath her and scoop her up.

"What...?"

"Easy, Hollywood." He gathered her close, stroked her hair, massaged her head.

She moaned. The massage felt good—or maybe it was simply human touch—but the pain still held her head like a vice.

"Hang in there a little longer. The medicine will kick in soon." He pressed his lips to her forehead, gently massaged her temples, her scalp, stroked his fingers over her closed eyelids and cheeks. Over and over again. He stroked and petted as though determined to telegraph with his touch that it was okay to give a little, to let him carry the ball for a while.

"Relax, sweetheart. Let me take care of you."

She curled into him. "It hurts. I hate to be such a baby."

"Shh. You can be anything you want to be with me." He shifted against the headboard, held her curled against him, her knees to her chest, her head on his shoulder.

The last person to take care of her was her mother, and that was ages ago. Steve had never even offered, which had continually surprised her, given that he was a doctor. She remembered him poking his head around the corner of their bedroom. *"Headache, huh? Sorry about that, babe. I'll be out late. Poker with the guys."* He never volunteered to even get her an aspirin or pull the shade.

And he certainly hadn't climbed in bed and held her as though she were a fragile figurine. As Chance was doing.

The care alone went a long way toward easing her, and Kelly could feel the drug pulling her into the healing sleep she desperately needed.

Chance kept up the rhythm of his fingers. Her breathing was evening out and he could feel her tense muscles relaxing. She was tough, mustered every last shred of control she had, fought any weakness as though it was an epidemic.

How long had she needed to be so strong? A young girl leading with her chin through medical school, a woman suffering through the dissolution of her family, the loss of a husband and her best friend, a mother moving to an unfamiliar place, to an unfamiliar way of life in a desperate effort to help her child.

Always alone. On her own.

He leaned his head back against the headboard, wondered if he had what it took to change that. He hadn't thought about a family of his own since that one disastrous relationship in medical school.

Now that was all he *could* think about.

KELLY OPENED HER EYES and glanced at the clock. Seven o'clock. She had no idea if that was morning or night.

Trying to move as little as possible, she assessed her condition and was so glad the horrible pain was gone she nearly wept.

Still a bit groggy and disoriented from the Demerol, she slipped out of bed and peeked through the blinds. The moon glowed like a spotlight against the snow-covered ground. Christmas lights strung along the eaves of the stable splashed prisms of color over the blanket of white.

Seven at night. She'd been asleep almost eight hours. How long had Chance stayed with her? Held her? Stroked her?

A funny tickle washed through her belly. He was the type of man most women only dreamed about. Strong, masculine and infinitely tender.

A man who would cherish the woman who became his.

He'd make someone a wonderful husband, and she felt a swift sting around her heart that it wouldn't be her.

Her life wasn't her own right now. It belonged to her children.

Even if that wasn't a problem, their worlds still weren't compatible. Everything she'd worked for was back in California waiting for her. She'd never planned to stay in Shotgun Ridge. She'd given herself until the end of December, a date that wasn't far off.

She'd made it clear from the start that her stay was only temporary.

After a long hot shower, she followed the scent of food to the kitchen, her stomach growling. Chance looked up when she paused at the kitchen doorway.

"Hey," he said softly. "How're you doing?"

"Much better, thanks. Once I'm able to get past the pain and sleep, the other medications go to work." She still wasn't sure how she felt about the intimacy of him taking care of her.

"Good. You know, it's usually customary to send flowers *after* someone's under the weather. If I'd known they were going to make you sick, I'd have sent them back."

She managed a smile. "Touch my flowers and I'll break your fingers."

He grinned. "At least I know you're highly quali-fied to fix them. Sit. Let me feed you."

"You're a bossy man, Chance Hammond." But she sat, anyway.

"Telling people what's wrong with them and how to fix it has gone to my head. I think I'm ruined for life."

Bossy *and* charming.

"Careful, this is hot," he said as he ladled beef stew

into a bowl in front of her. "You won't find better in the county."

"Modest, are we?"

"Hey, I've had plenty of practice. I've been a bachelor for a lot of years."

"And why hasn't some smart woman snapped you up?"

"Until recently I wasn't interested." He set crusty French bread on the table and sat down. "When I was young and idealistic, I fell in love with a city girl. I thought she shared my feelings, my vision for the future. Turned out she wasn't willing to settle in Montana. Especially in a small town."

"I'm sorry."

"Don't be. We both would have been miserable. It's a good thing we didn't rush and make a mistake."

She tasted the stew. It was fantastic. "It's nice that you're living your dream."

"That I am. What about you? You know why I do what I do. What made you choose child orthopedics?"

"I scrubbed in on a surgery that gave a little girl with cerebral palsy the ability to walk. It was incredible. She was incredible. Perhaps I gravitated toward children because I hadn't been much of a child myself. I don't know. Maybe deep down inside I thought I'd missed out on something."

"I can tell you right now you probably did."

She stopped with the spoon halfway to her mouth.

He grinned. "But that doesn't mean it has to stay that way. You're never too old to be a kid. Give us a little time. We'll catch you up."

His suggestion was so absurd she laughed.

He pushed his bowl away and leaned back in the chair. "It's good to see you laugh. That headache you had tore me up."

She gaped at him.

"I've never had a migraine, but watching you was vivid enough to have me imagining what it must be like. I hated to see you go through that."

This was getting dangerous. She decided to ignore the intimacy of his softened tone. "I wasn't all that happy myself."

"You want some more stew?"

"No, I'm fine. It was wonderful."

"Why don't we move to the den?"

"Shouldn't we do these dishes?"

"Later." He came around the table and held her chair, helped her as though expecting her to still be unsteady on her feet.

"I can manage, Chance."

He shrugged. "I'm a doctor. What can I say?"

Yes, and a doctor saw pain on a daily basis. So why had hers unnerved him? And why had his admission made her insides clench in both excitement and dread?

In the den he steered her to the sofa, eased her down as though she'd just been through major surgery and placed an afghan over her lap.

She wasn't used to this kind of treatment, but darn it all, she liked it.

When the fire was roaring behind the mesh screen, Chance sat down beside her, brushed aside her hair and looked into her eyes.

She smiled gently. "I really am fine."

"Have you been able to pinpoint what triggers the migraines?"

"No. It could be hormonal or stress or when my sleep cycle's messed up."

"And is it?"

"What?"

"Your sleep cycle messed up."

She shrugged. "Kimmy's nightmare the other night kept me up. Sometimes I think it's just my brain—thinking too hard. I go over every angle, come up with conclusions, then dismiss them because I'm scared."

"Scared of what?" His arm was over the back of the sofa, his fingers brushing her shoulder.

"Of pushing too hard. Of not pushing hard enough. I can't see inside her mind. This isn't a wound that I can look at and treat. It's not a broken bone that can be detected by an X ray. The psychologist who worked with Kimmy was a friend of mine, so I knew she was on the level when she said she'd done all she could do. To continue the therapy would simply be taking my money. She felt that Kimmy was close enough to me that if she was going to open up, it would be to me. As time passes, I'm not so sure she's right."

"Those girls love you."

"Yes, I know that. I just want this whole mess to be over."

"The kids were close to your husband?"

"No."

"No?"

She nearly smiled at the astonishment on his face, but the answer to his question was sad. "Steve was busy. He had a life pretty much separate from us. Oh, he loved them. But only on his timetable, do you know what I mean?''

"I have an idea. And I have to tell you, it doesn't endear the guy to me.''

"He wasn't that bad. Though I don't think I could have said that right after the funeral. Now that I've distanced myself from the betrayal, I do remember some of the good times.''

She pulled her knees up to her chest, her feet on the sofa, and wrapped the afghan more tightly. The warmth of the fire felt good against her back. She couldn't explain it, but the smell of pine and the twinkle of Christmas lights on the tree made her feel safe somehow, safe enough to open up about her life.

"I met Steve at a medical convention when I was twenty-four. He was ten years older and didn't seem intimidated by my being a doctor at such a young age. I hadn't had much experience with dating, and I was thrilled by the attention he gave me. We married and had Jessica right away.''

She toyed with the ends of her hair, feeling the sting of failure all over again. "The honeymoon period didn't even last through the pregnancy. We started drifting apart into separate lives. I had no yardstick with which to measure and figured that was standard— that married couples didn't have to live in each other's back pocket.''

"Independence is separate from romance, Kel.''

"Yes. I should have realized that by watching my own parents. I was busy, though, and fulfilled with my job, and we fell into a routine that I convinced myself was normal. Sometimes I felt as though Steve was competing with me, trying to prove that he was the better doctor, the better surgeon.

"Then he became obsessed with his looks, changed his specialty to plastic surgery and started hanging out with an elite crowd. When I came home at the end of the day, I wanted family time. I'd thought that's what Steve wanted, too. But he started staying out nights, always going to some party or benefit. Can you believe that I even encouraged him to go with Candy?"

He took her feet, drew them into his lap, rubbed his warm palms over them. She started to object, but it felt too good. His attentiveness continually caught her by surprise, encouraged her to continue, to talk about things she'd only discussed with one other person. Her father.

"Candy was my best friend. We met when we were both at UCLA. Candy was bouncing back and forth between art history and law. She had her cosmetology license and did hair and makeup to supplement her income through college. She sort of fell into a job doing celebrities' makeup on movie sets. It was Candy who introduced Steve to the world of movie stars. She was instrumental in putting him in the right place to launch his career in plastic surgery."

"Why do I feel as though you didn't agree with your husband's change in specialties?"

She shrugged. "It was his choice. I'd have respected him more if he hadn't been motivated by money. Plastic surgery is a valuable tool in medicine. Steve didn't take those kind of cases, though—you know, the cleft palates, burns and mastectomy rebuilding. He did face-lifts and liposuction on the rich and famous. That was it.''

''And made a name for himself.''

''Definitely. Which is what caused the media circus after he died.''

Chance, still massaging her feet, squeezed in compassion. ''And you didn't even have your best friend to turn to. Weren't there others? Friends?''

She shook her head. ''Because I'd been such a smart kid and so far ahead of the girls my age, I never really had girlfriends. Candy was the first. And the friendship meant a lot.'' She gave a self-deprecating laugh. ''I don't know much about the rules of friendship, but I do know that best friends don't steal husbands.''

''No, they don't. But the experience has made you wary of friendships...relationships.''

''What's that saying about once burned?'' She shrugged. ''Who knows? Maybe I'm not cut out for relationships. Some genetic flaw. Like the freak genetic makeup that made me what I am.''

With his hands at her ankles, he tugged and slid her right over into his lap. Surprise rendered her speechless.

''What you are is a caring, gifted, warm, compassionate, beautiful, sexy woman.''

That was a mouthful. She held her breath. Did he mean it? His expression said he did. She didn't quite know how to deal with compliments. Nor with finding herself in his lap once again.

''That's thrown you off, hasn't it?'' he asked, running the tip of his finger down her cheek.

She nodded. Couldn't yet speak. His thighs were warm beneath hers. What would he do if she shifted, straddled him, gave in to the combustible chemistry that continually simmered and sizzled between them?

"You're a woman who deserves compliments, Kelly. You deserve better than what you got from your marriage."

Oh, he said exactly the right things. She had an overwhelming urge to kiss him. Reaching up, she hooked her hand at the nape of his neck, applied the slightest pressure. In the back of her mind, she'd thought to express gratitude. While holding his gaze, it turned into something more. Much more.

For more than a month she'd been fighting the attraction between them, determined to keep her distance.

She wanted to give up the fight. It was too difficult to keep up the shield. They were alone for the night. She wouldn't be here much longer. School would start again for Jessica in January. Kelly was scheduled to begin seeing patients a week after that.

Once, just once, she wanted to feel this man's touch, wanted to feel like a woman. A valued woman. The sexy woman that he'd told her she was.

She wasn't sure which one of them made the first move. His head lowered and she met him halfway. She closed her eyes, felt the warmth of his lips, the sweep of his palm over her back, her hip, her thigh, over her rib cage and lightly, ever so lightly, against the side of her breast.

She turned into him, moaned, poured herself into a

kiss that tasted like every wish she'd ever thought to make.

Perfect. Coveted. So very right.

When he lifted his head, his breathing was as unsteady as hers. "We should slow down."

"Why?"

"Do you have any idea what you do to me? You make me want to take. But I watched you suffer through that headache a mere eight hours ago."

"Surely you've read the same studies I have. Sex is one of the best remedies for a headache."

He went absolutely still, studied her. A vein popped up on his forehead, testament to the tenuous control he held himself under. A log in the fireplace spit, sending a shower of sparks up the flue. Silence engulfed them for two heartbeats, then three.

"Are you sure? Be very sure, Kelly."

"I'm positive."

He stood with her in his arms, gazed down at her. His eyes locked on to hers, held her. "If you think this is only about sex, you're wrong. I'm going to make love to you. With you."

Oh, Lord. This was deeper than she wanted to go. But she nodded. Because she knew he was right. Their feelings were volcanic. They had been for a while now.

He carried her down the hallway to his bedroom, then slowly, carefully, slid her down the front of his body until her feet touched the floor. She remembered when he'd done something similar the night they'd decorated the tree. That time, her back had been to his front. This time, they were breast to chest, hips to hips and, at last, lips to lips.

He kissed her like a man desperate to quench a powerful thirst. His arousal was thick and hard behind the zipper of his jeans. He held her against him, shifting her from side to side, letting her feel his desire, torturing them both.

They weren't even undressed and she wanted to beg. But his mouth was fused against hers, his strong hands holding her right where he wanted her, controlling their movements.

"Chance," she managed when she came up for air.

"Mmm." His hands slipped beneath the hem of her sweatshirt. "It's been driving me mad all evening that you weren't wearing a bra."

She swallowed hard, drew in a swift breath when his thumb lightly stroked her nipple. In the lamplight, she could see the heat in his eyes, the intent.

He eased her down on the bed. "Let me build up the fire."

"It's roaring pretty good, if you ask me."

He chuckled and crossed the room to the stack of wood beside the hearth. In minutes a fire was crackling, throwing shadows over the hardwood floor and maple furniture.

When he turned back, though, he wasn't laughing. His gaze was intense, his steps determined. He was a man who knew what he wanted and wasn't going to beat around the bush or apologize for it.

It was the most exquisitely thrilling look any man had ever given her. It made her feel beautiful, sexy, as though she indeed had what it took to excite and fulfill a man.

Without breaking eye contact, he shrugged out of his shirt and tossed it in the corner. Kelly stood, intending to slip out of her clothes, too.

"Wait," he said. "Let me."

Stopping in front of her, he lowered his head, kissed her, then lifted her sweatshirt and pulled it over her head.

Kelly suffered a moment of embarrassment. The only man who'd ever seen her naked was Steve. And then it had been mostly in the dark.

There was plenty of light here. After giving birth to two children, her body wasn't as young and firm as it used to be.

He took her arms and uncrossed them, dropped to his knees in front of her, his gaze a warm caress as he looked up at her.

"You're so beautiful." His voice held a reverence that banished her unease as he removed her sweatpants.

Running his palms up the backs of her thighs, he cupped her behind, squeezed, pulled her closer and pressed his lips against the faint stretch marks at her belly, ran his tongue just above the elastic band of her silk panties.

Kelly gripped his shoulders for balance. "Chance..." She didn't know what else to say. Just his name.

"I know." He stood and lowered her to the bed, followed her down and fitted himself over her, using his knee to urge her legs apart. "Put your legs around me."

"Take off your pants first."

"Later."

Confused, she did as he asked, straining against him. Silk and denim still separated them. The sensual torture was incredible. His bare chest rubbed against her breasts. His hand beneath her hips lifted her higher and harder against him.

Kelly was certain she couldn't take the teasing, the anticipation. The need in her was too great, had been building for too long. She ran her hands over his shoulders, his back, to his tapered waist and the seat of his jeans, urging him to step up the pace.

He eased away, gently guided her hands to her sides.

"This time's for you, Kelly."

She frowned, not sure what he meant, but thought fled when he ran a fingertip down the center of her chest, slid his palm between her legs and cupped her. Her hips bucked. Chills raced over her skin. Chills of desire. A desire she'd never, ever felt before.

He was taking her on an incendiary, anticipatory journey that frightened her, but one she desperately wanted to take.

When his fingers slid beneath her panties to touch her, to delve inside, she thought she'd go mad. He gave, unselfishly, asking for nothing in return. She wanted to participate, but her limbs felt heavy, her mind blank except for the exquisite sensations coursing through her body.

Time seemed to stand still, to wrap them in a co-

coon of sensation, of discovery. With his lips and tongue and his body, he tasted and touched every inch of her, aroused her to the point of pain. She ached. Not like the ache of a headache. A pleasurable ache.

She sucked in a breath as his tongue drew a moist line over her abdomen. Slipping the silk panties down her legs, he kissed her in the most intimate way a man could kiss a woman.

"Wait..." The objection that came with her flash of uncertainty died in her throat. Not only had he introduced her to new Christmas traditions, he was creating sensual firsts. Extraordinarily sensual ones.

It was too much. And not nearly enough. Sensations raced through her system like a powerful drug. She couldn't hold a thought, couldn't catch her breath.

The fire crackled and popped. The orgasm that ripped through her drowned out sound. Nothing existed in that moment except Chance.

Pulling her hands away from his, she snatched at his shoulders, touched him where she could, her movements fevered, her body pulsing. She jerked open the snap of his jeans, unzipped them before he could stop her, shoved her hand inside and closed her fingers over the steel-hard length of him.

He sucked in a breath. "Oh, baby, wait—"

"No way." She rolled with him, took control. She wanted to climb right inside his body, feel all of him, experience all of him. She'd never, ever, had such a fierce desire to touch a man, to know him, explore him, consume him. She wanted to give him the same incredible pleasure he was giving her.

Denim chaffed against her bare skin. The teeth of

his zipper scraped against her thigh. She slid down his body, pulled off his jeans, then fitted herself over him, from neck to toes, touching, rubbing, aching.

His hands cupped her behind, pressed, rocked her against his straining arousal. Taking her by surprise, he rolled and swept her beneath him.

"I'm…" Her breath was coming so fast it burned her lungs. "I'm not through."

"And neither am I."

She looked up into his hot blue eyes. She'd pushed him to his limit. She could see that. Triumphant, she drew up her knees, opened for him.

He reached across her, yanked open the drawer of the nightstand and pulled out a box of condoms.

Kelly let out a feminine laugh she'd never heard from herself before. "A whole box?"

His mouth kicked up at the corners. "I figured we better make sure that headache doesn't come back."

"What headache?"

He smiled, then kissed her as though he wanted to absorb her right into his soul. Where before their movements were fevered, now they were gentle. "Hold on tight."

He entered her, filling her, sating her before he'd hardly even started. She couldn't explain the feelings washing over her in wave after wave of ecstasy. Was afraid to try.

Slowly, oh so slowly, he slid in and out, holding his weight off her, never taking his gaze from hers. Sensations built and it was all she could do to keep her eyes open.

He pressed high and hard, watched her.

He was following through on his promise.

This wasn't about sex.

This was making love.

Reverently, thoroughly, then with increasing tempo, he did exactly that. He made love to her, mind, body and soul. He took from her, but oh, he gave so much more in return.

Spellbound, he held her in a sensual trance, focusing his entire being on her pleasure. She could see it in his eyes, feel it in his movements, taste it on his lips.

He gave and he gave. And Kelly could only hold on as he'd asked, go along for the ride, flying on the wings of a desire so hot it scorched her from the inside out, squeezed her heart, changed her life.

He slid his palms beneath her, tilted her hips to meet his deepening thrusts. Digging her heels into the mattress, she met him, matched him, urged him on.

And like a rushing river sweeping her along without a will, she shattered around him, rode the crest of bliss as she felt him reach his own peak. What had taken place between them in this bed went beyond the realm of even her deepest fantasies, a joining that had touched her soul and laid her emotions bare.

She was afraid, so very afraid that she'd given up a part of herself that she'd never be able to take back.

That she'd never *want* to take back.

Chapter Eleven

One look at the clock and Kelly knew she was late. Very late. Chance was already gone and she'd overslept. Little wonder after the night they'd spent together.

Oh, Lord, she thought, her heart racing. Maria was likely to catch her in Chance's room. She flew out of the bed, snatched up her clothes and raced to her own room, where she showered and dressed in record time.

Coffee, she thought. Then a phone call to check on the kids. She'd have to go pick them up, which would put her at the clinic even later.

She pulled up short when she saw Chance in the kitchen, the coffeepot in his hand. A glance at the clock told her he was late, too.

"I'm sorry. I overslept."

The intimacy of his look warmed her. This was going to be awkward, she decided. It was the very thing she'd fought from the beginning, knowing that if they acted on the attraction between them, it would make it next to impossible to work side by side, day after day. Now what?

"Coffee?" he asked, standing there as though he

had all the time in the world. Which she knew he didn't. She'd booked the appointments for him herself.

"I need to call and check on the girls."

"I already did. I talked to both of them…well, Jessica talked for Kimmy. They wanted to stay longer. I said we'd pick them up this afternoon."

"I hate to impose on Hannah that way. And why aren't you at work?"

"I gave us the day off."

"You can't do that. You've got patients to see."

"Nope. When I went to get the Demerol yesterday, I brought home the appointment book. While you slept, I rearranged the schedule. If anyone has an emergency, they'll page me or use the radio." He brought her the mug of coffee, bent down and pressed a kiss to her lips, grinned when she drew in a breath and looked around.

"Where's Maria?"

"I gave her the day off, too."

"Why?"

"Because we're here. Alone."

"Chance…"

She'd yet to take a sip of her coffee. He took the mug back from her, set it on the table, drew her into his arms and kissed her. Her mouth automatically opened beneath his. He tasted of coffee and masculinity, and that alone quickly banished all her unease. The emotions rushing through her were simply too huge to ignore, to battle.

She was playing with fire, she knew it. Time was moving much too fast. Soon the clock would stop.

But for now, for as long as she was here, this man

was hers. They had the day off. Erotic possibilities were taking shape in her mind.

He lifted his head, stepped back.

"How about giving me a hand in the barn?"

"The…" She was still thinking about him taking her back to bed.

"You know, that building out there with hay and horse stalls?"

She narrowed her eyes. "I know what a barn is. What do you need help with?"

"The horses like to eat now and again, too."

She glanced outside. Snow was on the ground, but not falling from the sky. The bare branches of a willow didn't seem to be moving, so the wind wasn't gusting.

"Come on, Hollywood. You're not going to melt."

"I'm not worried about melting. I'm worried about freezing." But she grabbed her coat and scarf, and tugged on a pair of gloves.

Chance grinned and put the coffee mug back in her hands. He saw the flair of desire in her green eyes, but he'd seen the reserve that had preceded it. If he wasn't careful, she'd be pulling back, making excuses for why they shouldn't take their relationship to this next step. He wanted to make sure that didn't happen.

Holding the door for her, he waited until she'd stepped out onto the back porch. Brisk air bit at their cheeks. He saw her immediately start to bury her hands in her pockets, realize she was still holding a cup of steaming coffee and debate which she wanted more—caffeine or warm hands.

He took the mug from her and gathered her close to his side. "The barn'll be warmer."

"How can something that's so beautiful be so darn uncomfortable?"

"You get used to it. Encourages snuggling." *And sex.*

She slid her arm inside his coat and burrowed closer to his side, matching her steps to his. "I bet you deliver a lot of late-summer and fall babies."

"Actually they're pretty spread out." He glanced down at her. "We've been known to get snow in June, too."

"Are you kidding?"

"Nope." The expression on her face was so horrified he couldn't help but pause, bring her around to his chest and drop a kiss on her startled lips.

He'd miscalculated. He hadn't expected her to plaster herself against him. Even through several layers of clothes, his body responded to hers. Holding her coffee away from their bodies so he wouldn't spill it, he drew in a breath. "Maybe we should go back inside."

Now she was the one to grin, to tease. "And let Lolly and Peppermint starve? Uh-uh." She plucked the mug out of his hand and strode in front of him toward the barn. She'd show him she could handle a little cold.

As it turned out, she did more watching than helping. She knew nothing about feeding or caring for horses.

Scout was perched on a bale of hay, looking forlorn because the girls weren't there to play with him. Heaters kept the barn warm. The smell of damp hay, leather and animals permeated the air. They were unfamiliar smells, but tapped into something deep inside her nonetheless.

It was odd. She'd never been on a ranch before, yet it felt as though she had. Removing her glove, she stepped forward and ran her hand over Peppermint's soft nose, cheek and silky neck.

"Want to take a ride?" Chance asked.

Apprehension swamped her. "I don't know how. I mean, I've never ridden a horse before."

"I'll give you lessons."

For some reason the thought of him giving her lessons made her uncomfortable. She'd probably embarrass herself to death. Bundled up in bulky clothes, it was doubtful that she'd even be able to get up in the saddle without falling right back out. At least she'd be cushioned, she thought.

Still, she'd been weak in front of Chance one too many times for her peace of mind. First the mortifying possum incident, then the debilitating headache. She wasn't used to looking inept. And she didn't want to appear that way in front of him again.

"Come on," he urged. "You didn't skip high school and go into college without a healthy dose of gumption."

As dares went, that one was pretty blatant. She lifted her chin. "Saddle up."

He grinned. "That's the lady I'm so crazy about. We'll take an easy ride, keep it to a walk."

Although her heart leaped, she told herself not to dwell on that "crazy about" comment, even though he was looking at her like he expected her to.

"What if the horse has different ideas?" Peppermint looked sweet enough, but she was awfully big. And she didn't come equipped with a steering wheel or a brake pedal.

"I told you, Stony trained them well. I'll be right there beside you on Lolly, and Peppermint will do exactly what she does. Trust me."

Oh, she did. And for some ridiculous reason that made her want to cry. "Okay."

He handed her a brush. "Why don't you go ahead and brush her down, take a minute to get used to her."

She took off her other glove and put it in her pocket, then stroked the brush over the silky chestnut coat while Chance saddled Lolly.

"Don't be afraid to press hard. It feels good to her."

"Mmm, I imagine it does. Like a soothing back scratch, doesn't it, beauty," she crooned to Peppermint, sweeping the brush over the horse's coat and smoothing her hand behind it.

This wasn't so bad. And it did help to get close to the animal, relate to her up close and personal. Kelly felt an instant bond, and was surprised.

She stepped back as Chance came over to saddle Peppermint, then followed as he led both horses out of the barn. In the corral, he dropped Lolly's reins and placed a small stool beside Peppermint.

"Step up here and put your left foot in the stirrup, then use the saddle to pull yourself up."

"It won't slip off or anything?"

He grinned. "Promise."

She stood on the stool and he steadied her. "This seems like cheating. What if I fall off once we get out of the corral? I won't have a stool to get back on."

"You won't fall off, Kel."

She gave Peppermint a pat and hoisted herself up into the saddle. "Be patient with me, girl." When the horse shifted her weight, Kelly grabbed for the saddle horn, her heart racing.

"You're doing fine," Chance said as he adjusted the stirrups for her.

Feeling like a goalie on a hockey team with all these padded layers of clothing, she undid the buttons of her coat, then pulled on her gloves, hoping the horse wouldn't decide to move until she got a good hold.

Chance put the reins in her gloved hands.

"What do I do with them?"

"Very little. She'll mainly respond to your body movements. When you think about going left, your body will unconsciously lean that way. It's subtle, but she'll pick up on it. Give her a hand, though, and lay the reins lightly on her neck, and she'll turn whichever way you want to go."

"What about stopping?"

"Same thing. Just pull back gently. Don't worry, though. I'll be right beside you. After a few minutes you'll realize that Peppermint's taking you for a walk, and all you really have to do is sit there in the saddle and enjoy."

Well, if she fell out of the saddle, at least she was in good company—with a doctor. That thought was comforting.

With Scout trotting beside them, they left the corral at a walk. After a few minutes Kelly began to relax. The sensation of being on horseback was exhilarating.

Clumps of dried grass and brush poked through the

snow. Bare gray trees lined the frozen creek. No claustrophobia here, Kelly thought. For as far as she could see, there was wide open space and a sky that stretched forever. Off in the distance, cattle dotted the prairie and snow clung to fence posts.

"What do those cows do for food out here when it snows?"

"Right now, they can get to the grass. When the snow gets high, the ranchers will be out dumping hay daily."

"Do the cows stick together?"

"Mostly. Sometimes a few stray and have to be rounded up."

"I wouldn't want *that* job."

"It can get pretty miserable."

She glanced over at him. "You do it?"

"Sure. People aren't sick all the time. When I can, I help out the neighbors—mostly during spring roundup and branding. But there have been times a storm's moving in and the neighbors are shorthanded. Also times when someone's injured out on the range or caught in a blizzard."

"Don't tell me you make house calls—or outdoor calls—in a blizzard."

"Not intentionally. I've been caught a time or two, though."

"Chance, that's insane. You're the doctor. Shouldn't you take care of yourself so you can tend to others?"

"Out here, men don't go out in the elements without being prepared for just about anything. We're generally pretty safe. And there are plenty of line camps around if we have to ride out the weather.''

She rode in silence, thought about that. Chance's life here wasn't just about doctoring. He was part of the community, helped out wherever and with whatever he was needed for. Which included ranching and working on horseback.

A cowboy M.D.

Just looking at him sent a tickle through her midsection. He held Lolly's reins easily, sat tall and relaxed in the saddle. Thick, buff-colored gloves covered his hands. A fleece-lined denim jacket hung open over his chest. His black Stetson shaded his eyes, gave him a sexy dangerous look.

Her pulse skittered and her knees tightened on the saddle. Peppermint stepped up her pace, and Kelly whipped her attention back to what she was supposed to be doing.

''Whoa,'' Chance said, and maneuvered Lolly so that Peppermint immediately slowed down. ''Try not to squeeze your knees. She'll think you want her to trot.''

''I didn't mean to.'' That'd teach her to allow her mind to go off on a sensual tangent while sitting on horseback. But darn it all, the sight of the man beside her, together with the rocking motion of the animal beneath her spread thighs, was causing a throbbing awareness she couldn't seem to ignore.

A half-dozen hours ago, she and Chance had been making love. Her body was still sensitized and raring to go another round...or three.

As they walked the horses the perimeter of

Chance's land, the house, barn and corral were always in sight, an unobstructed view across the flat land. Smoke curled from the chimney. Patches of snow clung to the roof. Redbrick siding made a beautiful contrast to the landscape.

Kelly had always loved brick houses, but they didn't stand up well to earthquakes in California.

"You mentioned getting the girls a pet for Christmas," Chance said. "Have you thought more about that?"

"A little. But they haven't been hounding me for animals since they've had Scout and the cats to play with."

"I imagine that's going to change when they get home. The Malones have a litter of border collies that have just been weaned. When I talked to Jess on the phone, I think 'puppy' was mentioned about every other word."

Chance turned Lolly and headed them back toward the house. Peppermint smoothly followed, as he knew she would.

"I told Wyatt to watch and see which one the girls were partial to and save it for me. Figured I'd better clear it with you, though."

"So the puppies are old enough to be separated from their mother now?"

"Yes."

"Maybe we could go ahead and get it, then, and give it to them early." She looked at him a bit sheepishly. "I'm afraid I don't have any experience caring for a puppy and neither do the girls, but I imagine you could give us a crash course. If we wait until Christmas..."

Her words trailed off, but Chance didn't need her to finish the sentence. She planned to leave soon after Christmas. By the end of the year, she'd said. Christmas was a week from tomorrow. The new year a week past that. Not a lot of time to learn about the care of a puppy.

"We could do that," he said. "It'd be a gift from us, instead of Santa."

She smiled at him and he felt his heart skip. Man alive, this woman moved him. What would he do when she left? He'd never had a woman living in his home, never had someone to ride the property with, work with him, sleep with him, laugh with him. Now that Kelly and her daughters had permeated his life, how would he walk through the halls or travel these paths without them?

He had two weeks, he told himself. A lot could happen in fourteen days.

WHILE CHANCE FINISHED putting the horses away, Kelly remained outside, taking a deep breath of the bracing air. It wasn't really so bad, she thought, surprised. Or else she was getting used to the winter weather.

The sky was brilliantly blue with a few puffy clouds hanging low like giant cotton balls held aloft by an invisible wind. It was only midmorning, and she'd had very little sleep the night before, yet she felt energized.

Montana wasn't only good for her children, she thought. It was pretty good for her, too.

She was still staring at the sky in wonder when a snowball smacked her in the back with an audible *splat*. Astonished, she whirled around. Chance was already forming another missile. Before she could act, powdery snow hit her square in the chest, sneaking inside her coat, icy cold moisture dripping down her neck.

Stunned, it took her a moment to gather her wits. She saw the intent in his eyes, saw him gearing up to softly pelt her again. His movements were unhurried, nonchalant, like a lithe panther on the prowl, stalking, mesmerizing, moving closer.

His blue eyes locked onto hers like laser beams. His hat was cocked low, his cheek dimpled by a half smile that screamed sensuality, as well as devilish intent.

Well, he wasn't going to catch her off guard again. She scooped up a double handful of snow, packed it into a ball. Before her arm could rear back, another clump of snow glanced off her shoulder.

"This is war, Hammond." She hurled the snowball and dived down for another scoop, hardly taking time to pack it before she let it fly. She crowed and punched the air like a prizefighter when she beamed him on the forehead, nearly knocking his hat off.

"Not bad for a city girl." He wiped his face, but kept coming toward her.

It was thrilling in a dangerous sort of way. "We played a hospital softball game for charity," she said. "Much to my surprise, I excelled at pitching." She had another snowball in her hands and was backing up.

She ducked his next pitch and fired off two of her

own, laughing, shrieking. Switching tactics, she changed directions and charged at him, instead of backing away, flinging snow as fast as she could. She went to make a running pass around him, but she miscalculated.

He reached out and snagged her waist, taking her down in the snow with him, breaking her fall with his body. Laughing, freezing, she shoved against his shoulders. "No fair."

He winked. "All's fair in love and war, Hollywood."

The cliché was delivered in a teasing tone, but Kelly felt her heart stutter, then start up again with a vengeance.

The next thing she knew, they were kissing. His nose was cold against her cheek, his tongue hot in her mouth. He rolled on top of her, their legs tangling. Her arms went around him, knocking his hat off. Both vying for control, they rolled in the snow, angling this way and that in a frenzy of need and a frustration so keen Kelly actually whimpered.

Chance, on top again now, lifted his head and looked down at her. "All this exertion has made me work up an appetite. And there are way too many clothes between us."

She knew which appetite he was referring to. Her own hormones were leaping in an edgy, urgent way. "If we didn't have on this many clothes, we'd be freezing—or at least I would. I'm on the bottom."

"We can fix that." He stood and scooped her up in his arms.

The man moved faster than anyone she'd ever

known. "You know, we might have to talk about this tendency you have to cart me around."

"This isn't carting, sweetheart. It's carrying. There's a difference."

She grinned, because he was so indignant—playfully so—and endearing. And for the next little while, he was all hers. What did it matter who was taking control?

"I beg your pardon, Sir Galahad."

"And well you should."

Despite his teasing tone, the kiss he pressed to her lips was anything but. It was hot and tender, and sent her anticipation right through the roof. She wanted these heavy coats and clothes off. Now.

Chance pushed open the back door, remembered to lock it behind him. Setting her on her feet, he yanked off his coat, watching as Kelly did the same. Their movements were frenzied, as though fire ants had crawled inside their clothes.

He needed to get his hands on her skin. Slinging his gloves halfway across the kitchen, he snatched her to him, his palms sliding beneath her shirt, up her sides, pulling her sweater off.

He kissed her, his hands fevered. Pressing her against the ache in his groin, he held her there, rubbed her against him. It wasn't nearly enough. He unzipped her pants and pulled them off. Good thing she'd already kicked off her boots, or they'd have ended in a heap on the floor.

Cupping her behind, he lifted her. "Put your legs around me."

The position was even more torturous. She rode the

tip of his erection, a thin strip of silk and his denim the only thing separating them from sheer bliss. He didn't think he was going to make it down the hall.

"How do you feel about the kitchen table?" he asked against her lips.

"Like it's my new best friend."

"Thank God." He set her on the table, laid her back, yanked a condom out of his back pocket and slapped it on the maple wood, then closed his mouth over her nipple. Her back arched, exciting him, setting him on fire.

She fisted her hand in his hair. "Now, Chance."

"In a minute."

"No. I mean, I appreciate your consideration here, but can we save it? I'll let you go slow later."

Oh, man. He unzipped his pants, tore open the foil packet, rolled on the condom and entered her. He thought the top of his head was going to come off. Pleasure shot through him, his blood pounded in his ears. It was all he could do not to empty himself in her right now. He clawed for control as he pressed higher, harder, holding her hips steady so he could set the pace.

Her back was arched, her eyes closed, her nipples pebble hard. For all her special gifts, this woman hadn't had many new experiences. And each one of them showed on her face, the delight, the wonder, the passion. It made him want to give her the world on a velvet pillow.

He reached between them, touched her, and as fast as that, she came apart. Her climax was hard and strong. Each pulse of her body squeezed him, again and again. He held still, let her ride it out. It cost him a small part of his sanity, he was sure. But it was worth it.

Her breath heaved. "That was—"

"Only the beginning." He moved inside her, saw the stunned expression in her eyes, the immediate flash of pleasure.

"I don't think..."

"Oh, yes." He lifted her, his body still fused with hers and sat in the chair, feeling her glove-tight feminine muscles begin to pulse around him anew, squeezing, driving him right to the edge.

She grabbed the back of the chair, arched against him as he closed his lips against the side of her neck, inhaled the springtime scent of her perfume. He tried to hold her still, but she took his palms and guided them to her breasts. And with her hands over his, she moved against him, faster, harder. When she shattered around him for the third time, he gave up the erotic battle and let himself go.

Kelly collapsed against him, her heart nearly beating out of her chest. My God, she'd never felt anything like that in her life. She meant to tell him that, but she didn't think she had enough air to manage words just now.

Was that sex? she wondered. He'd said there was a difference. But it hadn't felt like just sex. Even amid their frenzy, her insistence that he save the consideration and slow touches for later, it had felt special.

He'd made damned sure of her pleasure before his own.

This man was so wonderful...so perfect.

Kelly didn't understand the sudden desperation that overcame her, the stinging urge to weep. Wrapping her arms around him, she held onto him with every bit of strength she had left in her body.

Her life was changing, spiraling out of her control. All because of a special doctor—Chance Hammond.

There was no turning back now. Her heart was involved. Deeply. Irrevocably.

She held him tighter, allowing her arms to convey the words she couldn't speak. And when she felt him grow hard inside her once more, she kissed him. A bittersweet kiss for the way life sometimes threw couples an insurmountable curve; for at last having found true love, but in the wrong place and at the wrong time. It simply wasn't fair.

"Kelly?" Chance pulled back, searching her gaze.

"Shh. Don't talk. Just make love with me."

His expression softened into a tenderness that *did* bring tears to her eyes.

"Yes," he whispered against her lips. "We'll make love."

Chapter Twelve

As Chance had predicted, all Jessica talked about for the next two days was the puppies at the Malones. Kelly knew Chance was making arrangements for the surprise, and despite herself, she was nearly as excited as she imagined the girls would be.

In the meantime Kelly was in the kitchen baking cookies for the church cookie exchange and social that was supposed to take place later that evening.

She wasn't a baker, could probably count on the fingers of one hand how many times she'd even attempted it. But she was excellent at following instructions, and Maria kept a slew of cookbooks in the cupboard.

Kelly could have asked the housekeeper to do the baking, but she really wanted to do it herself. It was important, though she wasn't sure why.

"You girls are going to eat up all the cookies, and we won't have any left for the exchange." Kimmy had a ring of chocolate around her mouth—Kelly was majorly impressed with herself over the excellent results of *that* batch of cookies—and Jessica had sugar all over her from the gingerbread men and traditional Christmas cookies.

The kitchen looked like a flour bomb had exploded in it, but she and the girls had never had so much fun.

She lined up the tins she'd bought in town and using wax paper, layered them with cookies.

"What's that noise?" Jessica asked.

Kelly looked up, listened. Someone was singing.

Several someones.

"I don't know. It sounds like a choir." After wiping her hands on a towel, she took off her apron and lifted Kimmy down from the chair. "Come on, let's go see."

Chance, who'd been stealthily wrapping gifts in one of the back bedrooms, met her in the living room, grinned and opened the front door.

Kelly was speechless. It looked as though all their neighbors and their neighbors' ranch hands, too, were standing at the bottom of the porch steps, singing Christmas carols.

Carolers.

She'd seen people do that on television, but never experienced it in person. She'd thought it was just a nice story people told.

Chance lifted Kimmy in his arms and held out his hand for Jessica. Stepping out onto the porch with them, Kelly noticed that the yard was filled with hay wagons, sleds, horses, a couple of snowmobiles and a few pickups.

"Oh, my gosh." This was Christmas, she thought. She felt giddy.

Memories of her grandmother taking her to the historic district of Los Angeles to walk the streets and look at the spectacular light displays swam in her mind. Those were rare and special times.

This was...this was so real. So genuine. So perfect.

She folded her hands in front of her mouth, felt emotion clog the back of her throat. Eden Stratton strummed a guitar, the fingertips of her mittens cut away, as Stony stood beside her, singing in harmony and holding their baby daughter. Ethan Callahan's brother, Clay, played a harmonica.

Hannah and Wyatt Malone stood arm in arm, as did Ethan and Dora Callahan. Cheyenne and Emily Bodine, each holding a twin bundled in heavy blankets, stood beside them. It seemed like everyone had a baby in their arms. Most of the faces in the crowd she recognized, some she didn't.

"Oh, this is wonderful."

"We do it every year," Chance said. "One family starts it. As they're invited into their neighbors' homes, they talk each household into joining them, and they go from there, increasing in numbers. By the time they get to my house, it's practically the whole town."

Kelly wanted to be part of this. Without hesitation. Without thought. She wanted to join in.

With giddy excitement, she listened as her friends and neighbors sang the last refrain of "Silent Night," all the while her brain planning, organizing. Thank goodness she had extra cookies and a pot of cider simmering on the stove.

She clapped when they finished the carol, and

opened the door wider. "Come in and warm up," she said to the group, laughing for the sheer joy of it.

When she saw the gentle smile on Chance's face, she suffered a moment of embarrassment because she was acting like this was her home, instead of his. She got over that quickly enough. He'd told her to treat the place as if it was hers. And besides, no one seemed to think a thing about it.

Amid hugs, handshakes and goodwill, the house filled with bodies clad in heavy coats, scarves, wool caps and Stetsons.

Eden strummed a few chords on her guitar, warming up the crowd for more singing. Kelly instantly forgot her hostess duties and sat down at the piano, listening. Finding the key, she began to play and joined in on the chorus of "Jingle Bells."

Everyone clapped, surprised and delighted with the additional music—and that Kelly was the one providing it.

When the song ended and Clay went right into a lively rendition of "Grandma Got Run Over by a Reindeer," there were plenty of groans, laughter and children's giggles.

Kelly's fingers faltered. That piece wasn't in the Christmas sheet music she'd unearthed from inside the piano bench.

Concentrating, determined to make an attempt, she hit a couple of off-key notes, laughed at her blunders, then found a choppy rhythm. Her recital teacher would have cringed. Several weeks ago Kelly herself would have cringed. She rarely did anything less than perfectly—other than shooting trash cans.

But imperfection was incredibly freeing...and fun.

This is what Chance had been talking about. What she'd been missing. Community spirit. Friendships. Joining in.

Fun.

"Wait till Pastor Dan finds out how well you play the piano," Dora said when the lively song came to an end. "He'll be recruiting you for Sunday services."

Kelly laughed. Never mind that she wouldn't be here for enough Sunday services to take over the job of pianist, she wasn't going to let anything dampen her spirits tonight. "Which one of you are going to tell on me?"

Innocent looks abounded, yet that didn't mean a thing in Shotgun Ridge. No doubt the preacher would be informed by the time the group reached town.

"Are ya'll ready to go?" Eden asked. "We'll carol at Brewer's, then head on over to the church for the cookie exchange."

"If you don't have cookies, Eden has enough to go around for all of us," Emily said. "And don't feel bad. She did my baking for me."

That was because Emily had brand-new twins to deal with, Kelly knew, which didn't leave her a lot of time to spend in the kitchen. "I baked," Kelly said shyly, inordinately proud of herself.

Chance gave her a smile she couldn't decipher. Pride? Love? "You get the goodies. I'll bundle the kids."

Kelly fairly ran into the kitchen, snatched up the tins, turned off the burner under the pot of cider and was back in the front room in record time. It seemed as though everyone was talking and laughing at once. The festive air gave her a warm tickle in her stomach. These people were here for her, waiting to include her in their community. Well, not only her. They were here for Chance, too.

The camaraderie, the inclusion, made her heart burst with joy. This was such a new experience. And she planned to embrace it with both arms, accept the joy into her heart.

Chance held the tins of cookies as she slipped into her coat, then reached over and lifted her hair out of the collar, his fingertips resting against her neck for a moment longer than necessary. The intimacy was obvious to her, and probably just as obvious to everyone else in the room who cared to look.

"Quit it," she whispered, but he only grinned and slung an arm around her as they followed the neighbors out of the house.

They couldn't have picked a more beautiful night for caroling. The sky was filled with a million stars. Even the moon couldn't dim the vast, diamondlike blanket overhead, a sight one couldn't see in the city.

Kelly glanced at the snowmobiles in the yard, then at the vehicles, several powered by engines and others by animals. The couples with young babies piled into the pickup trucks. Chance led her to the hay wagon, and Kelly was thrilled.

"How will we get back home if we don't take our own car?"

"Same way we get to town." He lifted her into the back of the horse-drawn hay wagon Wyatt Malone was piloting, then handed up each of the girls and vaulted in beside them.

Bells jingled as the horses began to walk, then broke into a trot. Kelly wanted to laugh from the sheer joy of it all. With her arms around both of her daughters, she sat between Chance's splayed thighs, her back leaning against his chest, and joined in singing "Frosty the Snowman."

Jessica belted out the words with little regard to tune, and Kimberly rocked her head in time with the rhythm. Chance's deep voice lifted above them, his arms warm where they wrapped around to encompass all three of them.

Just like a family. His family.

Kelly experienced a moment of sadness that this would all come to an end very soon.

"Sing, Hollywood."

She leaned her head back, looked up at him. "I am."

His gentle eyes chastised her. "You're thinking too much. This isn't the night for that."

"I know. Thank you," she whispered.

"For what?"

"For this." She indicated the wagon, bales of hay, the neighbors and the countryside with a sweep of her hand.

"I'm afraid I can't take the credit. This is a Shotgun Ridge tradition."

"Not everyone adheres to tradition."

He pressed his lips to the top of her head, said quietly, "*I* do. Always."

Kelly linked her fingers with his, pulled his arms

more securely around herself and her daughters. This man was nothing like her late husband.

This was a man who'd be content to stay home at night, who'd carry half the load or more without question or qualm. Who'd never balk at a simple family dinner when there was an invitation for a fancier do waiting on the hall table. A man who truly enjoyed people and the season for who and what they were, instead of what they could do for him.

A man a woman could trust implicitly with her heart.

"KEEP THE KIDS outside for a minute," Chance said when the Malones dropped them off at home several hours later.

Kelly nodded and watched him jump down off the hay wagon. She knew what he was up to. During the cookie exchange at the church, Chance had slipped out with Skeeter Hawkins, Wyatt's foreman, to retrieve the puppy Jessica and Kimberly had fallen in love with. Kelly had watched them leave and return, both men wearing pleased looks on their faces. Skeeter Hawkins had the bowlegged gait of a man who'd ridden a horse all his life. He'd been the foreman on the Double M since Wyatt had been a boy. The old man could still outrope any cowboy around. And he was a sucker for little girls and playing Santa Claus.

Jessica and Kimberly exchanged hugs with Ian and Nikki, and made plans for the next sleepover. Kelly worried that the kids were spending too much time at other people's houses and decided they should invite Nikki and Ian to stay *here* next time.

They were building so many new traditions, cementing relationships—falling in love...*all* of them. And though it was wonderful, it was also dangerous. It would only make the parting more difficult.

"Where's Chance?" Jessica asked when the hay wagon rolled out of the yard, bells jingling.

"I think he went inside," Kelly said, barely able to keep her excitement in check. "He probably got cold. Shall we go see?"

She took each of the girl's hands in hers and mounted the porch steps. In the living room, the lamps were low, the Christmas lights on the tree lit and sparkling like gemstones.

Beneath the tree in an open cardboard box was a tiny black-and-white border collie pup, a huge red bow tied around its neck.

"Snowball!" Jessica shrieked, charging across the room, nearly knocking Chance over as she reached to scoop up the little dog. Kimmy, eyes wide and delighted, ran to join her sister. She looked up at Chance, then at Kelly, hope shining in her round eyes.

"Is he ours? Really and truly?" Jess asked.

"Yep. All yours. And Kimmy's, too." Chance said. "Merry Christmas, girls."

"Oh, thank you, thank you!" She hugged the puppy. "Kimmy, look! Mommy, look! He's 'zactly the one we wanted!"

"I see," Kelly said, coming to stand beside Chance. The girls both got down on the floor, lavishing love and pats on the excited puppy.

She looked up at Chance. "He is pretty cute."

"The runt of the litter. But he's healthy."

Trust her children to choose the most needy of the bunch.

Chance pulled Kelly over by the fireplace and tugged her down to the floor where they could watch the girls frolic with the puppy.

"I can't believe they already named him. What if we hadn't gotten him for them?"

"Are you kidding? Those girls know darn well they've got us wrapped around their fingers."

Kelly smiled. "Shameless, isn't it."

He ran a fingertip over her cheek, smoothed her hair behind her ear. He was so close, his gaze so intense, so...loving. Kelly had an urge to step away, but Chance seemed to read her intent and pulled her closer, draping his arm around her shoulders, holding her back to his chest as he leaned against the couch.

Jess suddenly giggled when the puppy skidded on the quilted tree skirt, then sniffed at the string of popcorn hanging from a low branch. "Look, Kimmy! Marcy patted him on the head."

Kelly nearly groaned. "I'd thought a puppy would replace the imaginary angel."

"And you're so sure she's imaginary?"

"Oh, for..." She looked at him, saw his smile. "You're a good man, Chance Hammond."

"Yeah, I keep telling you that."

She shook her head, gave his thigh a whack. He covered her hand before she could draw it away, pressed it against his denim-clad leg.

"How come the kids haven't had a pet before now?"

"Steve didn't want animals in the house."

"You married a guy who didn't like animals?"

"I didn't know he didn't like them."

"Hmm. Guess the kids had to make do with their friends' pets, then?"

"Not too many of those, either. Friends, that is. Jessica went to a private school and none of her classmates lived nearby. All of this is very new to them—sleepovers and outside activities. Actually it's taking some adjustment for me to accept that they always want to spend time away from home."

"It's good for them. It's normal and natural for kids to want to get away from their parents, to spend time with their peers. Besides, Santa's got to have some privacy to do his thing."

"Santa did a pretty good job tonight." She snuggled closer to his side. "Thank you."

"You're welcome. Again."

She smiled, lulled by the heat of the fire and the festive Christmas lights and the joy of her daughters playing with their new puppy.

If she hadn't been in the Christmas spirit before, she was definitely in it now. She'd never looked forward to, nor dreaded, something so much in her life. She wanted to experience it all, soak it up, revel in the atmosphere.

But with the holiday would come an end. When the gifts were unwrapped and the lights came down, it would be time to leave. To go home.

Later that night, in Chance's bed, she snuggled into his arms, held him tight. Even though he assured her the intercom system would pick up the sound of the girls if they needed her, she never spent the whole night in his room. But each night she stayed longer and longer, reluctant to let go.

He tucked her beneath him, raised above her and stroked her hair back from her temples. "What is it?" he asked softly.

Tears stung her eyes. She might have known Chance would tap into her emotions. He was so attuned to her. She shook her head. "I have to go back to my room. But, just for another minute, would you…would you just hold me."

And he did. "For as long as you'll let me, sweetheart."

AT THE CLINIC they saw the usual colds and flu, but other than that, business was starting to slow and Kelly was barely even working part-time hours. That was fine with her. She'd only intended to fill in for a few months, anyway. Chance really should be advertising for a nurse.

Today, though, Chance talked her into going on his house calls again and Kelly didn't refuse. The kids were so enamored with their puppy, they hardly seemed to even know when Kelly was home.

After gathering up food and toys, they headed out to the trailer park outside town.

"Are you going to play Santa?" Kelly asked him, glancing back at the boxes of supplies and goodies in the back seat.

"The holiday gives me an excuse to help out. These people are proud and hate to take charity. This is my way of trying to make a little bit of a difference without stepping on their pride."

"Is someone in the household sick?"

"Lanette's one of my regulars, more of a complimentary checkup just to stay on top of things. She's in her late twenties and has two kids. You know how quickly they can pick up and pass along germs."

She nodded. From the time her own girls had entered day care, then kindergarten for Jess, it had been one bug after another.

They came to a stop in front of a single-wide trailer perched sadly on small patch of land with clumps of weeds poking up through the muddy snow. Kelly retrieved the box of food, diapers and wrapped gifts, while Chance grabbed his medical bag.

A young woman held the door open as they went through, giving Kelly an uninterested glance. A boy of about two clung to her skirt.

"Hey, Doc Hammond. I wasn't expecting you today."

"I told you I'd be around, Lanette."

"I musta forgot. I been doing that a lot lately."

Her skin had an unwashed look. Anemia, Kelly suspected, rather than dirt.

"This is Dr. Kelly Anderson," Chance said. "She works at the clinic with me."

"Pleased to make your acquaintance, ma'am," Lanette said and led them into the kitchen where a baby lay sleeping in a bassinet in the small dining alcove that apparently doubled as a nursery. The linoleum floor was discolored and buckled, and dishes were piled in the sink. Grains of toast speckled the margarine tub where someone had been too impatient to clean off the knife.

"How are things?" Chance asked.

Lanette sighed, sitting at the fifties-style dinette table as Chance checked her eyes and the glands in her neck. The metal rim around the Formica surface was popping loose, and the brown floral plastic covering the chairs was taped in places to hold in the stuffing, but the surface was relatively clean.

"I'm just so tired all the time."

"Do you have help with the kids?" he asked. The smell of urine from a pile of soiled diapers in the corner permeated the room. Two yellow dogs lay on the worn carpet, heads on their paws.

Kelly had never been exposed to this side of life, and she wasn't sure how to react, so she kept quiet and simply watched.

The young woman shrugged. "Dody helps, but he's got his work, you know. And I just don't feel like doing…*it,* so he says how can I expect him to want to help when I don't want to do it."

Kelly realized the woman was talking about sex. Chance obviously figured out the same thing.

"That's normal when you're feeling tired." He had his stethoscope just inside the button front of her shirtwaist dress, listening to her heart. "How old's the baby now?"

"Three months. Dody said I shoulda been better at six weeks."

"Some women take longer." He put the stethoscope back in the medical bag. "Do you want me to talk to him?"

"Oh, no! It's just…" She hesitated. "Sometimes I

just want to lay down and not get up.'' Tears welled in her eyes.

Chance patted her knee. ''I can give you a vitamin shot, have you start taking some iron supplements.'' He squatted in front of her, took her hands in his. ''Have you heard of postpartum depression, Lanette?''

Eyes rimmed in dark circles widened. ''I heard about a woman over in Idaho who killed her babies because of that. I'm a good mama, Doc. I'm not gonna hurt my babies.''

''I know, Lanette. The medicine I'd like you to try will just balance the chemicals in your body, put a little sunshine back in your step.''

She looked away. ''The good Lord knows I could use a little more spring in my step, but we can't afford no extra expense for medicine. We need the money for the kids.''

''It won't cost you a thing. We get free samples from drug reps all the time. I'll just run them out to you.''

Lanette brightened. ''You can do that?''

''Sure.''

Just like with Barney Heppermill, Kelly knew the cost of the medication would come out of Chance's own pocket.

Not wanting to intrude, Kelly stood back and watched him finish up with Lanette, then coo over the little boy and the baby, examining them and passing out toys and food, taking a moment to play and visit and giving every impression that doctors all over the world dispensed Christmas gifts as a natural part of their service.

He was an amazing man, Kelly thought. An amazing doctor. Tall and strong and sexy and compassionate.

And with her heart melting right there in the shabby kitchen, Kelly fell in love with him all over again.

This was the worse mess she'd ever gotten herself into.

Damn it, she was going to break her own heart, and she had no way to prevent that from happening.

Chapter Thirteen

The next day, with Jessica and Kimberly in tow, Kelly headed toward King's Western Wear to do some last-minute shopping.

She'd used the Internet to make most of her purchases for the girls. It still gave her pause not to have all the conveniences she'd always taken for granted—malls around every corner, mailboxes every two blocks.

In Shotgun Ridge, UPS picked up and dropped off at Tillis' General Store. A trip to pick up her purchases meant half a day of visiting, as everyone and their sister, it seemed, wanted to stop and talk and discuss what was in the packages. Nosiness didn't even enter into the equation. Friendship did.

It was something Kelly was starting to look forward to. In California she was merely a number at the post office; here she was greeted by name and welcomed with big smiles.

"How come Snowball couldn't come with us?" Jessica asked for the twentieth time.

"Honey, Snowball's still little. He's not crazy about cold weather and he likes to stay in his nice warm basket. Besides, he doesn't have any money to spend.''

''We could give him some.''

''If we'd brought him, then he'd know what you bought him for Christmas. You want him to be surprised, don't you?''

''Well, don't get mad at *me* if he eats the popcorn on the tree,'' Jessica said with an innocent look.

Kelly sighed. The puppy was worse than a baby. And in her daughters' eyes, he could do no wrong.

''I'm sure Maria will keep him away from the tree.''

''Uh-huh.'' Jessica shared a look with Kimmy, and Kelly didn't even try to decipher it. ''Where are we going now?''

''To buy a gift for Chance.''

That perked her up. ''Can me and Kimmy get him something, too?''

''Of course.''

''And for Nikki and Ian? And...'' Jessica took a moment to think, then named off half the people in town and their pets, too.

Kelly realized her gift-giving list was growing considerably. But instead of worrying about it, she embraced it, enjoying herself. Past Christmases had been harried. She'd almost resented having to go out and choose gifts.

This year she felt different. There was a spirit of giving and goodwill that she'd never known before.

Even during the daytime, the town was festive. It was too early for the lights to be on, but windows and doorways sported wreaths and painted glass and colorful displays.

King's Western Wear shop had a Santa in the display window wearing a cowboy hat and pointed-toe leather boots. Bells jingled above the door when they entered, and Jessica and Kimberly immediately spotted Mildred and Opal Bagley. Thrilled, they raced across the room to the widows, who happily enveloped the girls in hugs and kisses.

"Land's sake," Mildred said. "I've missed having you sweet baby dolls staying at my house. How are things out on the ranch?"

"We got a new puppy! His name's Snowball and he got borned from Lady—that's Ian's border collie. Chinook's a boy doggy, so he can't have babies, but that's okay. Snowball's just little. Skeeter said he was a runt. But I don't think he's a runt. He's so be-au-teeful!"

"Well, then," Opal said. "I'm certain he's just perfect. Isn't it the luckiest thing that you've got all that room on Dr. Chance's ranch." She included Kimberly in her greeting, gently caressing the little girl's cheeks.

"Yep," Jess said, eyes shining. "And Marcy loves him, too, and she likes the ranch."

"Marcy?" Mildred asked.

"For heaven's sake, sister," Opal chided. "I do worry about your brain. How could you forget Marcy, the angel?"

"Oh, worry about your own brain, Opal."

Opal sniffed. "If you weren't so obsessed with your silly fingernails, maybe there'd be room in that gray head of yours to keep up with the residents of our town."

"At least I have fingernails."

Kelly bit her lip to keep from laughing. An imaginary angel was hardly a resident of the town. It had taken some getting used to, the way these sisters openly bickered over the craziest things. And they did it mostly for show, to raise an eyebrow, distract or simply entertain.

They were absolutely lovely.

"Kelly," Opal said, "you're positively glowing. Ranch life appears to be agreeing with you, too."

"It is—not that it wasn't delightful living in town at the boardinghouse with you all."

"You'll stop by sometime on Christmas Eve, though, won't you? We'll be serving a bit of cheer—hooch for Mildred," she said in a stage whisper, "and cider and cocoa for the children. We've gifts to pass out, too."

"We'd love to stop by."

"Wonderful," Mildred chimed in. "And don't let sister kid you. She nips into the hooch more than anyone. It's a wonder she can even walk a straight line to the bathroom—which she uses more than the rest of us, I'll have you know."

Kelly did laugh then. "It's so wonderful to see you both. You're taking care of some last-minute purchases?"

"Just finished up." Opal rolled her eyes. "Sister's been rushing me like an old woman bent on pushing through the pearly gates. She's got an appointment over at Arletta's to get those ridiculous little Christmas trees touched up on her fingernails. Fake, every last one of them."

"Well, we've company coming in tomorrow," Mildred defended. "At least I'm feminine enough to pay the beauty shop a visit and look my best. If you'd let that shorn hair grow out a bit like Arletta's been urging you to, you might feel a touch feminine yourself."

"And then where would we be?" Opal argued. "We'd both be primping, and not a lick of work would get done at the inn."

Mildred snorted.

Kelly decided to head off the conversation before there was bloodshed. "Who's coming in?"

"Eden's folks. Wonderful people. Beverly's a judge and Sam is a chef. Delightful, both of them. And there's other happy news. Emily Bodine's mother and stepfather are coming to town. Not to stay at the boardinghouse. They'll stay at Cheyenne and Emily's. Isn't that just wonderful? It was Emily's fondest hope that her mother would come around and be a grandmother to those sweet babies."

"Yes, I remember. That's fabulous news."

"Well, we've kept you from your business long enough. If we don't scoot, Mildred will miss her appointment and I'll never hear the end of it." Both sisters hugged and kissed Kelly and the girls, then went out the door, tugging on hats and gloves and linking arms companionably as though they hadn't been sparring for the past ten minutes.

Feeling as though she'd been caught up in a comedic whirlwind, Kelly spoke to King Johnson, the owner of the store, and browsed through the merchandise, allowing the girls to select their own gifts.

For Chance, they chose a new bandanna, a pair of

gloves and a belt buckle. The dogs got bandannas too, and Nikki and Ian some fuzzy earmuffs.

Just for fun, Kelly and the girls tried on cowboy boots, and when Jessica and Kimberly had streaked off to play with the saddles and feathered hatbands, Kelly quietly asked King to set aside the boots. She'd be back later to pick them up.

She was examining a pair of leather gloves that her father might like when Ozzie Peyton came in the door.

"Ought to get you a cowboy hat to go with them gloves, you bet."

Kelly smiled. King's Western Wear was getting as busy as the General Store and Brewer's. "The gloves aren't for me. I was thinking about them for my dad."

"Right nice pair. Looks like a perfect fit to me, you bet. Won't find better anyplace else."

"You've talked me into it, then." She placed the gloves on the counter with the rest of her purchases.

"So what do you hear from Bill?"

Kelly had an idea Ozzie Peyton heard from her father more often than she did. Ozzie and Bill Dunaway had served in the war together—Ozzie a belly gunner, Bill a medic stationed at the same air base. It had been Ozzie that Bill had contacted when Kelly was looking for a change, a place to spend the holidays and step back from the turmoil in her life.

"He's flying in on Sunday."

"Cutting it close. That's the day before Christmas Eve. Need me to run over to the airport and fetch him?"

"No, he said he'd rent a car."

"Well, that's good. Looking forward to seeing him

again, you bet. Still hard to believe he gave up his medical practice to dabble in them computers.''

''Those computers have made him a bundle.''

''And you became the doctor in the family.''

''Yes.''

''A good one, I hear tell. Bill brags on you.''

Kelly smiled. ''It's embarrassing sometimes.''

''Nonsense. If a daddy can't brag on his girl, then the world would be a sad place.''

A sad place, indeed, Kelly thought. Steve had rarely bragged on his daughters. He'd been too busy hobnobbing with the elite.

But Chance bragged. And the girls weren't even his daughters.

Lord, there had been so many changes in her life she hardly recognized herself. Had it been only since late October that she'd arrived in this magical town? Become part of it?

How was she ever going to leave?

''DON'T GO POTTY on the rug,'' Jessica admonished the little dog. Tongue hanging out, he gave her such a cute look Kelly decided she'd be happy to clean up any accidents. How in the world could they even think of scolding such an adorable little ball of fluff?

She sighed. She'd always been a terrible disciplinarian with the girls. Thank heaven they were blessed with naturally good dispositions and a willingness to obey the rules. Otherwise they'd probably be on their way to delinquency at the ripe old ages of six and four. She imagined she'd be just as bad with the dog.

As Jessica had warned earlier, the puppy had

chewed the popcorn off the bottom branches of the tree. They were going to have to get a gate and fence it off—or pay closer attention to Chance's instructions on training puppies.

With newspapers spread all over the floor in Jessica and Kimberly's bedroom, Kelly tucked the girls in to the double bed and Snowball into his box. Scout hopped up and made himself comfortable on the quilt, giving the puppy a look of superiority.

"Can Snowball sleep with us, too?"

Kelly looked at the little dog. He stood on his hind legs, his black-tipped front paws hanging over the lip of the box. "I don't know…"

"Dogs in the bed," Chance complained fondly from the doorway. "You've spoiled them rotten and they'll never be the same." He scooped up the puppy and tucked it between the girls. For several minutes there were giggles and barks as animals and children—and Chance—played and goofed around.

"Okay, settle down everyone," Kelly said. The five occupants on the bed gave her a look that clearly stated she was a killjoy.

"Mom's right. Better mind or we'll all be in trouble."

After hugs and kisses, including the dogs, Kelly and Chance turned off the lights and headed back to the living room to finish wrapping gifts.

"I'm a sucker for big round eyes," she said.

Chance raised a brow. "How about mine? Are they big and round enough?"

"Is that one of those wolf questions?"

He laughed. "I'm crazy about you, Hollywood."

"Yeah, well, get to wrapping, or Santa's gonna get caught with the goods."

"Slave driver."

"You're worse than they are, you know. What if Snowball piddles in the bed?"

"I'll put him back in his box after everyone's asleep." He reached over and stuck his finger on the ribbon she'd wrapped around a box, holding it in place so she could tie a bow.

"Thanks. Will your family be coming out for Christmas?"

"No. They alternate. This year they're spending Christmas with my sisters, but everyone is coming out here for New Year's Eve. I'd like you to meet them."

Kelly wasn't sure that would be possible. Perhaps she could delay her trip home just a bit. A couple of days, maybe. Because she'd like to meet his family—especially his mother. She wanted to compliment the woman personally on her incredible paintings. And she wanted to buy and have one shipped to her.

Mentally making plans to leave was depressing her.

"Your one sister's name is Lisa. What's the other's?"

"Allison."

"So how'd you come by your name? It's not exactly commonplace."

"I'm the youngest. They named me Chance because they were taking one last chance to have a boy baby before they quit at their agreed-upon limit of three."

"Ah. I guess I shouldn't be surprised. Your mom's a creative person."

"That she is."

"What's it like having a famous mom?"

"I don't think of her as famous. She's just my mom. She baked cookies and cheered at football games and pitched a fit when she found out I was the one who drove the pickup truck through the Langleys' field and inadvertently got Emily Bodine—she was a Vincent then—hauled in for being underage and out after curfew."

"You were a bad boy."

"Of course not. I was charming."

She laughed. "Your modesty astounds me."

"Yeah, but you love it."

Her hands stilled on the ribbon. Their gazes met. She nearly agreed with him, caught herself.

Standing, she took the box and placed it under the tree.

He came up behind her. "Why do you do that?"

She didn't pretend to misunderstand. "Because I'm scared."

He put his arms around her, drew her back against his chest. "It's okay to be scared. Just don't pull away."

"Chance—"

The phone rang, startling them both. Kelly looked at the clock. It was only nine-thirty. Not really that late. But calls at night usually meant Chance was needed at someone's house.

She watched him pick up the phone from the end table, then frowned as he held the receiver out to her.

"It's for you. A Dr. Laura Gorman."

The partner in her practice.

Kelly took the receiver, sat down on the couch. "Laura, how are you?"

"I hope I'm not calling too late. I didn't think about the time difference until I'd already dialed."

"No. It's fine. It's still early. Is everything all right?"

"Yes. Actually it's great…from my end, anyway. I'm not so sure how you'll feel about it."

"What's up?"

"I've been offered a professorship at UCI Medical Center as head of their children's orthopedics department."

"Oh, Laura, that's wonderful. Are you considering it?"

"I've accepted, Kelly. That's why I'm calling. It's what I've always wanted, and it's a great honor to be asked. The position starts after the first of the year. I guess I just needed your assurance that you were going to be back by then."

That had been the plan all along. So why did she suddenly feel so odd? She glanced at Chance, who was standing by the fireplace, staring at the flames. His back was to her, but he was obviously hearing her side of the conversation.

"It'll mean that some of my patients will shift over to you," Laura said, then paused. "Kelly? You *are* coming back, aren't you?"

"Of course." *Oh, God.*

"Listen to me. I'm a horrible person for not asking right away. How are the girls?"

"Thriving."

Laura paused. "Montana's that good for them?"

"It seems so."

"And Kimmy?"

"No words, but she's starting to resemble the little girl she once was."

"That's terrific news," Laura said gently. They were partners and friends, knew about each other's lives, but they weren't the kind of pals who shared every secret and socialized a lot outside of work.

"You know, kiddo, I realize you wanted to ease up on your caseload when you came back, and with that in mind I took the liberty to talk with a couple of colleagues who've expressed an interest in joining the group—Michael Leland and Stephanie MacNiel."

"From San Diego?" Kelly asked. She knew their reputations. They were excellent surgeons. It would definitely boost her career to align herself with them.

"Yes. I'm pretty sure they're willing to make the move to L.A. I can set up a meeting with them if you want, but it really should be you doing the interviewing, since you'll be working with them…won't you?"

It was all so much to think about. Here she was geared up for Christmas, experiencing things she'd never experienced, becoming part of a community, falling in love, watching her daughters laugh and smile and frolic.

Damn it, she'd acquired a puppy.

All of which she never should have done since she'd *known* her time here was only temporary.

But life had intruded. Fate had intervened.

Chance Hammond had happened.

And now reality had reared its head to smack her in the face, to remind her what was at stake. A lifetime of work. A career. A five-year lease on an office building that would be a huge financial burden if she walked away from it.

Perhaps in the back of her mind she'd thought that Laura would always be there to handle the practice. To be honest, Kelly hadn't done a lot of thinking lately. She'd only been going with the flow, enjoying, living in a dreamworld.

A regular Scarlett O'Hara worrying about tomorrow when it came.

It had come.

"Why don't you do the preliminary interviews, Laura? I'll touch base with you after Christmas." Three days. Kelly's heart felt heavy in her chest. Three days to decide. Three days to say goodbye.

She took a breath. "Laura? Congratulations, sweetie. This is a terrific honor, and you deserve it."

"Thanks, Kel. Merry Christmas. Give the girls a hug."

"I will. Merry Christmas to you, too."

She hung up the phone and looked up. Chance was watching her.

"Problem?"

It shouldn't be, so why did it feel like it? "Not really. That was my partner. She's been offered a professorship at a teaching hospital."

"Where does that leave you?"

Her smile was forced, she knew it. But she had three days. This was her time. Hers and her daughters. She'd wanted a new experience, a special holiday. She was going to enjoy it.

She felt she should apologize to Chance. But for

what? Her career? "It leaves me to scramble for another partner for the group."

He was watching her closely. She saw both resignation and respect. Chance wasn't a man to compete like Steve, to begrudge an opportunity. He was too self-assured. Too special a man.

"You have a lot to think about," he said quietly.

She went to him then. "Right now, I have Christmas to think about. And gifts to wrap."

The heat of his body radiated toward her, tempted her. She put her hands on his shirtfront, her eyes pleading for him to understand, to not make it more difficult. It wasn't fair, what she was asking of him.

She had an idea that she knew his feelings, though she couldn't be absolutely certain. He'd never professed to love her. Never actually asked her for a commitment. For long-term. He'd respected her need for distance.

He'd never asked her to give up anything for him, and she didn't think he ever would.

The only thing on which she was absolutely certain was that her heart would break when she left.

But what choice did she have? She had obligations. A lease in her name. Patients. An entire life in another state.

He slid his hands over her shoulders, her arms, stroked up and down, warming her with the essence of his body, his touch, his soul.

"What do you say we call it a night?"

She nodded and slid her arm around his waist as they shut off the light and walked down the hall.

Three more days. If she could, she'd pack a lifetime into those three days.

Chapter Fourteen

After church the next day, Kelly spent the rest of the morning getting one of the guest bedrooms ready for her father's visit. He was due that afternoon, and she was excited. Aside from the girls, he was all the family she had left...except for the extended family she'd acquired here in Shotgun Ridge.

A pang of sadness swamped her. Everything was changing so fast. Ever since the phone call last night, she and Chance had been walking on eggshells, both avoiding talk of the future, both knowing what it held.

The girls had picked up on the tension and were bickering more than usual—Jessica vocally, Kimberly in actions.

Kelly sighed. She had to do something to break the strain. The last thing she wanted was to ruin their lovely holiday.

She heard glass shattering, then Jessica's scream. "Mommy!"

Running down the hall, her heart pumping, Kelly skidded to a halt in the living room. Chance wasn't far behind her.

Kimmy stood frozen by the tree, a shattered glass

angel in splintered pieces at her feet. She looked terrified, as though she expected punishment for something that was an accident.

"Oh, baby, it's not your fault," Kelly said. It was the most heartbreaking thing in the world to watch a four-year-old with tears streaming down her plump cheeks and no sound coming from her trembling lips.

Kelly picked up her daughter and held her away from the glass, tried to infuse her with love, with the strength of her arms. She felt so impotent. Such a failure.

Jessica, ever protective of her little sister, watched from several feet away, a sadness on her face that was too old for her years. Kelly remembered a time when the kids fought over every little thing—the color of M&M's, doll clothes, toys, attention…everything.

But when Kimmy's voice had disappeared, so had any hint of dissension between the girls—except for a couple of times today, perhaps.

For the most part, Jessica was patient and sweet with her little sister. Too patient and sweet for a normal six-year-old.

"It's okay," Kelly crooned, including Jessica with the soothing words.

Chance scooped up the puppy and put it in its box so there wouldn't be cut paws, shooed Scout out of the way, then stooped to sweep up the broken glass.

Neither one of them was prepared for the bombshell Jessica dropped next.

"It's all my fault that Kimmy can't talk," she wailed, barely able to speak through her sobs. "I said mean, bad things to her after you yelled at Auntie

Candy. I told Kimmy it was her fault Daddy died, 'cause she didn't call you.''

At her sister's admission, Kimmy buried her face in Kelly's neck, and Chance immediately swung Jessica up into his arms, soothing her with a hand on her back, rubbing, patting, consoling.

"Oh, Jess." My God, Kelly thought, she'd been concentrating on Kimmy because her problems were obvious. She should have known better, pushed harder to draw Jessica out.

"I said I was sorry!" Jessica sobbed. "I told her and told her and *Marcy* told her, too! But she won't *believe* me!"

"Oh, honey." Everyone was walking around with a load of guilt and blame. Including Kelly. It was time to unburden.

With Kimmy in her arms, she sat on the couch and motioned for Jessica to join them.

Chance, his heart nearly breaking, brought her over. His arms felt empty as she climbed into Kelly's lap and settled, tears dripping off her chin.

Two little girls clinging to their mother. He wished he could help, wished he could wave a magic wand and make it all better.

"We need to talk about how Daddy died, okay?"

Jess nodded. Kimmy remained stoic, trapped in icy shock and her world of silence.

"I'll leave you alone," Chance said.

Kelly glanced up as though she'd forgotten he was still in the room, a ravaged look on her face. "Stay. Please."

He nodded. She needed support. He didn't know if he could give it, but he wanted to try.

"Electricity is a wonderful thing," she began, stroking her daughters with fingers that trembled. "It runs our lights and our televisions and radios and many other things. But we have to respect it, be careful. Daddy knew that, and he was always careful. He had no reason to suspect that the tool he was using in Aunt Candy's garage was broken. It was old, sweeties, and it malfunctioned—it didn't work like it was supposed to. That was nobody's fault. I know I yelled at Aunt Candy, but I didn't mean it. I was scared, and just like you did, Jess, I said bad things."

"But you're a doctor. You said you could fix him."

"No. Even if I'd been right there in the garage, I couldn't have fixed him, Jess. The electricity hurt his heart."

"Why?"

What she was asking was why did he have to die. Chance had heard the question before. There were no easy answers.

"It's hard to say," Kelly whispered. "We don't know why sad things happen. Maybe it's like one door closing so another, nicer one can open. Something happens and everything we thought we knew changes."

Jessica plucked at the thick yarn on her sweater. "It changed when we comed here and lived with Chance and got Snowball and got to play with Scout and Nikki and Ian."

Kelly looked up at Chance. Was he the door they were supposed to walk through?

"Yes, there have been nice changes."

"Do you think Daddy's sad?" Jessica asked. Kimmy lifted her head, listening intently.

"No. No one is allowed to be sad in heaven."

"Is Daddy an angel?"

That'd be a miracle. "Marcy, you mean?" Was this what was behind her insistence on seeing an angel? A coping mechanism?

"No, silly. Marcy's a girl angel. She's not Daddy."

"Oh. Well, I suppose Daddy could be an angel. I do know that he's probably watching over you, and he would never, ever want either of you to be sad or think you were to blame in any way."

Jessica nodded and Kelly felt Kimmy relax against her chest.

Then Jess reached over to hug her little sister. "I'm sorry I yelled at you, Kimmy. You're the best sister in the whole wide world."

Jessica's compassionate little voice had Kelly swallowing back tears. She couldn't fall apart or she'd undo any good she might have managed to accomplish.

Kimmy hugged back, then linked hands with her big sister.

"Does everyone feel better?" Kelly asked. "Understand that none of us are to blame for what happened to Daddy?"

Both girls nodded and scooted off the couch to resume their play with the dogs.

Kelly wished she could be distracted so easily. She felt raw, turned inside out.

Chance came over to her, brushed the hair back from her temples.

"You okay?"

"No."

"Ah, Hollywood." He drew her into his arms. She shouldn't let him, should find the wherewithal to raise her shield.

She'd been looking at life differently since she'd learned what true intimacy was like. How in the world was she ever going to leave all this behind?

But what else could she do? She had a partner counting on her, a thriving medical practice. Everything she knew was in California. It was ridiculous to feel as though she belonged here in Montana.

Her future was so sketchy. She couldn't make any plans or decisions, couldn't take anything for herself. Her children came first. She couldn't predict if Kimmy would heal, or if something would set her back and send her deeper into the pit of whatever it was that held her—Jessica's careless words or the horror of what she'd seen.

"How could I have missed Jessica's torment, too?"

"You're only human, Kel."

Oh, but she needed to be so much more. Had always needed that.

She hadn't been enough of a mother to keep her youngest from traumatic symptoms. Maybe the therapist was wrong. Maybe Kimmy didn't feel close enough to her, didn't trust her enough. And that was her own fault. For not being there, for spending longer hours in her medical practice than she should have.

Well, she would be there for her children from now on. Their needs would always come first.

Or so she thought. The instant her father knocked on the front door several minutes later, the second she looked into his loving hazel eyes and melted into his arms, her own needs swamped her.

"Daddy." Just that. Just the one word nearly sent her into an embarrassing bout of weeping.

"How's my best girl?" Bill Dunaway leaned back to look at her in concern.

She sniffed. "A mess."

He lifted a brow, but she shook her head. "We'll talk later, okay?"

"Grandpa!" Jessica shrieked. Both little girls took a running jump and leaped into their grandfather's arms. Despite his age he was a big man with muscles he kept honed at the local gym with the help of a personal trainer. He easily fielded both kids with a single swoop.

"Hey, it's my other two best girls."

"Grandpa, we got a puppy!"

"You did? Well, let me get my bag inside and you can introduce me."

"I'll get it," Chance said. He carried the suitcase over the threshold, set it down. "I'm Chance Hammond."

"Pleased to meet you," Bill said. "I'd shake hands but they seem to be filled with granddaughters at the moment."

"Chance has horses, too!" Jess began to chatter the second there was a break in the conversation. "We rided on Peppermint. And Lolly's a'scared of rabbits, so we can't hop around her. And wait till you see Scout and Maria and Nikki and Ian and...and *everybody!* Ian's doggie is the mommy of Snowball. Oh, Grandpa, I'm so *happy* you're here. The Christmas tree talked to us and— Watch out!''

Bill, about to move into the room, came to an immediate halt. ''What?''

''You almost stepped on Marcy!''

He looked around, puzzled. ''Marcy?''

''The angel,'' Chance and Kelly said in unison.

Kimmy looked incredibly pleased that they seemed to be able to see the same thing she and her sister obviously did.

Kelly felt a little silly encouraging the fantasy. Chance appeared perfectly okay with it, and Bill fell right into step without batting an eye.

''I beg your pardon, Marcy.''

Kelly sighed when her father gave her a wink and a curious look. She'd have to explain later. ''Jess, give Grandpa a chance to settle in before you talk his ear off. He's had a long trip.''

''Jess and Kimmy, why don't you come out and help me with the horses?'' Chance suggested.

''Can Snowball come?''

''It's a little cold for him, and he looks kind of sleepy. Scout can come, though.''

''Okay,'' Jessica answered for both of them.

Kelly gave him a grateful smile. Her nerves were strung pretty tight as it was. And she'd enjoy the opportunity to visit with her dad for a few minutes alone.

Chance took the girls outside and Kelly got her father settled in a guest bedroom, then brewed a pot of cinnamon coffee and sat down at the kitchen table. Snow wasn't falling, but the clouds were heavy in the sky, threatening to open up.

"Did you have any trouble getting from the airport?"

"No. Ozzie gave me good directions."

"I imagine you're anxious to see him. We'll be getting together tomorrow night for a Christmas Eve celebration over at the church."

"I'm more anxious to know what's going on with you. And with that cowboy doctor who was looking at you like you hung the moon and stars just for his benefit."

"Oh, he was not."

Bill reached over and placed his hand on top of hers. "This is your old dad you're talking to here."

She glanced at him. "Can't put anything over on you, huh?"

"Nope."

"It's complicated, Dad."

"Life usually is. You've fallen in love, haven't you."

She jerked, sucked in a breath, started to deny. One look at her father and she knew it was no good.

"I got a call from Laura," she said, instead. "She's accepted a teaching position at UCI."

"And that's a problem?"

"Oh, I just don't know." Before she could censor her thoughts or words, she found herself pouring out her feelings—about this town, these people, about the practice waiting for her in California...and about Chance.

"I didn't mean for any of this to happen, Daddy. I knew it was only temporary."

"If you return to an all-new practice, new dynamics, it'll thrust you back into even longer hours. Isn't that what you were trying to get away from in the first place by coming here?"

"In part, yes. Frankly, I think I was grabbing at straws, clutching a fantasy-type ideal as though it would hold the answers to the questions I didn't know I wanted to ask."

"And does it?"

She shrugged. "What have I really accomplished, Dad? Our time here has been wonderful, but Kimberly still hasn't spoken."

"She's coming out of her sad little shell, though. Surely you see that. I do, and I've been here less than an hour."

"So what are you saying? That I shouldn't go back?"

"Honey, I can't make that decision for you."

She stood, went to the window and gazed out at the corral where Chance and her daughters laughed and horsed around. "What if I asked you to?"

Bill went to her, put his arms around her, hugged her close. "The day you ask someone else to make a decision for you is the day the world would probably come to a screeching halt, planets would collide. It'd be a big mess."

She gave a watery laugh into his shirtfront. "I've been stubborn all my life, haven't I. Did I put you and Mom through a lot of trials?"

"You've always been special, hon. Perfect. You

didn't put us through any more than any other loving family goes through." He kissed her forehead. "I've decided I'm going to go out on a limb here, though. Don't let Steve and Candy's betrayal color your life."

"I'm not!"

"Aren't you?" he asked quietly. "Second chances don't come along often. Be very sure before you close a door. A house or a medical practice can be sold or transferred. Love can't."

Her dad was sounding a lot like his buddy Ozzie Peyton, and Kelly wondered just how often the two pals had been communicating. And though he'd said he wouldn't tell her what to do, he'd subtly done just that, giving her his opinion. She had a lot to think about.

IT WAS CHRISTMAS EVE, a night filled with excitement, anticipation and a community spirit that was palpable in the pine-scented evening air.

And Chance felt like a damned coward. The feeling was new and foreign and he didn't like it a bit.

But he'd felt Kelly distancing herself for the past couple of days—since that phone call from her partner. Now that her father was here, Chance was giving her plenty of space, figuring that if he didn't confront her, she couldn't tell him goodbye.

Damn it, his heart felt like a lead ball in his chest. They were walking around on eggshells when they should have been celebrating the season, laughing, enjoying...loving.

Once again he was reminded of his fiancée who'd chosen big-city over small-town life with him. The fact that he hadn't fought for Dana or compromised was an indication that he hadn't really been in love, after all.

What he'd felt for Dana was nothing like the gut-wrenching, breath-stealing feelings he had for Kelly.

Standing around the twenty-foot-tall town tree, surrounded by friends and neighbors, he assessed all that he had—his home, his friends, a medical practice he loved.

Could he go back to doctoring in the city? Leave all this behind?

The answer came to him in a heartbeat.

For Kelly he would.

"Is Santa gonna come here?" Jessica asked, distracting him.

"He already has. See the presents under the tree? That's why we come over here to the church. In Shotgun Ridge, before Pastor Dan preaches his Christmas Eve sermon, Santa always leaves one gift under the town tree for each girl and boy in town."

"What about for the mommies and daddies?"

"Naw. That'd throw his schedule off too much. You see, while the kids are opening their gifts here, he flies off to the neighboring towns to make other deliveries and give us enough time to go to church, then get home and in bed again before he lands on our rooftop to slide down our chimney. The man must be exhausted, don't you think?"

Jessica looked at him solemnly. "He prob'ly gets tired, but he has magic."

"Mmm. I'm sure he does." Chance looked over at Kelly. What passed between them was surely magic.

It had been from the first moment he'd laid eyes on her. And he didn't ever want to lose it.

He wanted to hold her, *insist* that she stay with him, give him a chance, give *them* a chance. The turmoil in his gut nearly sent him to his knees.

As Dan Lucas led them in a chorus of "Joy to the World," Chance gave in to the urgency of his needs, drew Kelly to his side. Her voice stilled.

And when she looked up at him, it was the most natural thing in the world to press his lips to hers.

In this, there were no barriers between them. The chemistry was blinding, binding. He loved her more than he ever thought humanly possible. She was his soul mate, the woman who completed him. And if he let go, she might so easily slip through his fingers. He couldn't let that happen. *Wouldn't*.

Around them, neighbors sang and rejoiced. And Chance kissed her with a desperation he wasn't used to feeling, trying to infuse her with all the love bursting inside him. Could he make her stay? Or convince her to let him come with her when and if she left?

The sudden silence around them brought his head up. He felt a tiny hand slip into his and looked down at Kimberly.

Something wiggled inside her coat. Then Snowball poked his head out just above the top button.

He grinned, but the expression froze on his face an instant later.

"Look," Kimmy whispered.

It seemed as though the world stood still at that moment. He was afraid to breathe. Afraid not to.

He dropped to his knees, ignored the puppy licking

his chin, glanced in the direction Kimmy pointed. There, standing off to the side, was a figure in glowing, flowing white. He shook his head, questioning his eyesight.

Could he be seeing Marcy? The angel the girls insisted was real? It wasn't possible.

Around him, the crowd buzzed in shock and surprise.

"Did you see that?" someone gasped. "What was it?"

"Just a flash of light," someone else responded, though with little conviction.

But Chance had the oddest notion that it was much more than a mere flash of light. The girls' guardian angel had put in an appearance.

At that moment, though, Chance had eyes only for Kimberly Anderson. Kelly was on her knees beside them.

"You spoke," he said, emotion clogging his throat, his heart pounding with joy.

"Uh-huh. The angel said I could."

As simple as that. She had a sweet, little-girl voice that hadn't lost its baby tone.

He hugged her to him, looked at Kelly. She was openly weeping and laughing, wrapping her arms around both of them.

Kimberly had spoken. Kelly had accomplished what she'd set out to do by coming to Shotgun Ridge. Now what? His heart hammered. He couldn't give her up. Couldn't give up these children.

"Kelly..."

Kelly lifted her hand to his handsome face. Her

heart was wide open. She knew his thoughts. She'd spoken often enough about her reason for being here and her intention to eventually leave.

A miracle had occurred tonight. Or maybe it had happened the moment she'd stepped foot in this wonderful town.

But something else had happened, too. In only a few months she'd fallen in love, learned what it was like to be protected, to be revered, to be treated like a lady, to have her vulnerabilities celebrated. Even to accept that she didn't always have to be perfect.

And in that short span of time, her child had been healed—by the love of a special doctor and the love of a town.

The choice between her life in California and the cowboy M.D. she'd fallen in love with became clear at once.

Before now, Kelly had simply never considered staying. She thought her home was in California. Frankly, when she'd come to Shotgun Ridge, she'd never dreamed she'd want to stay. It had never entered her mind that this could become permanent.

Drastic changes were what *other* people made. Kelly had always settled for what was in front of her— life as she knew it.

Well, that life was no longer recognizable.

This one here with Chance was.

No mansion or seven-figure income or Beverly Hills medical practice could compete or compare.

She cupped his face, then pressed her lips to his, unconcerned that an entire town watched them with bated breath.

"Is there room in this town for two doctors?"

His blue eyes flared with caution, hope and love. "I imagine so. If the matchmakers keep at it, the town'll be expanding into the next county."

"Want to be my partner?" she asked.

"Define partner."

"Drs. Chance and Kelly Hammond of Shotgun Ridge, Montana."

"Are you asking me to marry you?"

"I am."

He snatched her to him, kissed her long after it was proper, long after the need for air pressed upon him. Then he drew back and looked down at Jessica and Kimberly, who were grinning like Cheshire cats. Happy little girls. With *two* voices.

"What do you say, girls?"

"You should say yes," Jessica advised primly.

Kimberly nodded her head. "Snowball says so, too. You could be our daddy."

Oh, man. He looked back at Kelly, never realizing he could feel this much joy. "Yes. My answer is definitely yes. I love you, Kelly. I love these girls. You won't be sorry. I promise."

"I know. I love you, too. I never knew what love really was until I met you."

He wanted to rush, make sure this wasn't a dream, claim this woman as his wife and these precious children as his daughters. "Let's get married tonight. Everyone's here."

"I think we need a couple of days to get a license."

"Judge Lester would pull some strings. I'll give him free medical exams for life."

She laughed, pressed her hand over his heart. "New Year's Eve," she promised. "That way your parents and sisters will be here, too. I never knew how much family and friends could mean. I want to be part of it all. With you."

"I love you, Kelly." He kissed her. With his heart and his soul, he promised her the world with the simple, loving sketch of his lips.

And as friends and neighbors clapped and cheered, snowflakes fell from the sky like feathers from an angel's wing. His voice filled with emotion, he whispered, "Merry Christmas, Doctor."

OZZIE PEYTON slapped his old war buddy on the shoulder, his eyes wet with emotion. It didn't matter who saw. Age and wisdom and his sweet Vanessa had taught him there was no shame in honest emotion.

And there was plenty of that on the church lawn tonight as he watched Chance pledge to Kelly and those sweet little girls a commitment for a life together. Why, the love between them was bright enough to melt the snow right off the branches of the town tree.

And to think that he and his buddies and the man beside him—Kelly's father—were pretty much responsible for it all gave him a nice warm feeling.

Yessiree. Against the backdrop of a white Christmas in Montana, this was the season of miracles where anything was possible—love, an angel and the sweet voice of a silent child.

The good Lord was lookin' down on them for sure—though sending an angel was a bit risky, seeing as a shock like that could jolt a man into cardiac arrest, you bet.

The star atop the Christmas tree glistened, a wink of light that snagged his attention and made his heart settle contentedly in his chest. It was a sign. He knew just where to look for them.

You done good, Vanessa. I was only half jokin' when I asked you to speak to the Man Upstairs. Merry Christmas, my love.

*   *   *   *   *

Next month it's Dan Lucas's turn!
Don't miss Mindy Neff's
final installment in her
BACHELORS OF SHOTGUN RIDGE
miniseries.
906
PREACHER'S IN-NAME-ONLY WIFE
Available January 2002
at a store near you.

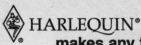

CALL THE ONES YOU LOVE OVER THE HOLIDAYS!

Save $25 off future book purchases when you buy any four Harlequin® or Silhouette® books in October, November and December 2001,

PLUS

receive a phone card good for 15 minutes of long-distance calls to anyone you want in North America!

WHAT AN INCREDIBLE DEAL!

Just fill out this form and attach 4 proofs of purchase (cash register receipts) from October, November and December 2001 books, and Harlequin Books will send you a coupon booklet worth a total savings of $25 off future purchases of Harlequin® and Silhouette® books, AND a 15-minute phone card to call the ones you love, anywhere in North America.

Please send this form, along with your cash register receipts
as proofs of purchase, to:
In the USA: Harlequin Books, P.O. Box 9057, Buffalo, NY 14269-9057
In Canada: Harlequin Books, P.O. Box 622, Fort Erie, Ontario L2A 5X3
Cash register receipts must be dated no later than December 31, 2001.
Limit of 1 coupon booklet and phone card per household.
Please allow 4-6 weeks for delivery.

**I accept your offer! Enclosed are 4 proofs of purchase.
Please send me my coupon booklet
and a 15-minute phone card:**

Name: _____

Address: _____ City: _____

State/Prov.: _____ Zip/Postal Code: _____

Account Number (if available): _____

---

097 KJB DAGL
PHQ4013

Coming in December from